K.C. MCMILLIAN

Loving Reign

A FAKE DATING ROMANCE STORY

Kiana (K.C.) McMillian

<u>*NOTE:*</u>

*Please be aware that this book contains sex, foul language, mentions of cancer, and family trauma.
It is recommended for mature audiences 18+ and older.*

For more details regarding content warnings for this book please visit my website: https://kcmcmillian.mailchimpsites.com/

To my family members and returning readers who purchased this book to support me, I want to express my heartfelt thanks for your continued support.

To all new readers, welcome! Thank you so much for taking a chance on my book. I hope you enjoy reading about Reign and Dion's journey to love as much as I enjoyed writing it.

Thank you for joining me on this ride and supporting me as an author.

Dedication

This is for all those who enjoy a little spice in their lives and a happily ever after!

Table of Contents

Chapter 1: Reign 1

Chapter 2: Reign 11

Chapter 3: Dion 27

Chapter 4: Reign 39

Chapter 5: Dion 47

Chapter 6: Reign 56

Chapter 7: Dion 66

Chapter 8: Dion 72

Chapter 9: Reign 80

Chapter 10: Reign 88

Chapter 11: Dion 96

Chapter 12: Reign 107

Chapter 13: Reign 114

Chapter 14: Dion 119

Chapter 15: Dion 129

Chapter 16: Reign 134

Chapter 17: Dion 146

Chapter 18: Dion 158

Chapter 19: Reign 166

Chapter 20: Reign 180

Chapter 21: Dion 188

Chapter 22: Dion 194

Sneak Peek: Book Two 203

Chapter 1: Reign 204

Author's Note 211

Books by K.C. McMillian 212

Acknowledgments 213

About the Author.. 216

Thursday
October 24th, 2024

Chapter 1: Reign

I'm in a *fake* relationship with Dion Atom James—yes, you read that right! *The* Dion Atom James, the child star from the peanut butter commercial where he became an overnight sensation by licking his lips, rubbing his belly, and saying, *"Yum, that's good!"* Yes! That guy! He's grown into a handsome and talented actor, maintaining the same charming smile that made us all fall in love with him as kids. I still can't believe it, but here we are, preparing for my younger sister's wedding rehearsal dinner, with a few unexpected twists and turns along the way.

As I check my appearance in my floor-to-ceiling mirror, I see Dion walking up behind me, looking dapper in his tailored black tuxedo. The sweet smell of sandalwood fills my nose as he approaches me. He rolls his broad shoulders back, and his light brown eyes meet mine in the reflection. My stomach flutters like a swarm of butterflies brushing against my insides. He surprises me by gently draping a rose gold necklace around my neck, its intricate design sparkling in the sunlight streaming through the window. What could this mean? My heart drops to the tip of my toes, and I gasp at his fingertips brushing against my skin as he fastens the clasp, igniting a rush of blood to my most sensitive area. The mere touch of his hand has me wet and seeping through my panties. I want this man inside me right here and right now!

One thing's for sure: This fake relationship is starting to feel a little too real. He's an actor, after all, so he knows how to play his part convincingly. But the way he's looking at me right now, with such intensity and tenderness, makes me wonder if there's more to this charade. He mentioned that he needed to discuss something with me; however, we agreed to talk about it after my sister and her new husband wedding nuptials. How did this happen? How did we get here?

Before we dive into the juicy details of my current situation with Dion, let's backtrack a bit to where it all began.

Wednesday
May 8th, 2024

Beep-beep-beep.

My alarm goes off, and I spring into my morning routine. I live in a one-bedroom, one-bathroom penthouse on the prestigious Upper East Side of Manhattan. My home features an airy living and dining area with oversized windows and hardwood floors that I can slide up and down in my socks.

The chef's kitchen is open-concept with granite countertops and stainless-steel appliances, but all I know how to do is boil ramen noodles and cook scrambled eggs. Yeah, I know, pathetic, right? To have such a beautiful kitchen and not know how to cook is beyond me. Perhaps I should add cooking lessons to my to-do list. Anyway, there is a full bath with a washer and dryer in the unit. Down the hall is my bedroom, with a walk-in closet big enough to fit all my clothes, shoes, purses, and an elegant accent chair. Purple is my favorite color, so I decorated the space with fig and grape hues, as well as silver accents, to add a touch of glam.

Is it evident that I'm happy to call this place home? I worked damn hard to be able to afford it, so I take pride in my cozy abode.

I refused to use my trust fund because I wanted to prove to myself, my father, and, most importantly, my mother that I could afford a place of my own, although it took me several years to save enough money to make it happen.

Then, when I could finally afford it, I used some of the money from my trust to buy furniture; my father complimented me on my resourcefulness. My dad is one of the top pediatric surgeons in the tri-state area, and he loves what he does. Granted, he missed a lot of my childhood, like some of my basketball games, but I'm a daddy's girl at heart, and his approval means everything to me.

Oh wow! I'm rambling, and I haven't even gotten to the best part yet. My name is Reign Amara Brown. There's a significant meaning behind my middle name, but we'll get to that later. Now, where was I? Oh, right, the best part! I'm a brown-skinned queen standing at five feet nine with a tiny waist, a lot of sass, and some ass. Do you see what I did there? Well, I got it from my momma! The ass, not the sass. That's just about the only thing I got from her. Do I seem conceited? Maybe a little, but I'm confident in my skin…or at least I try to be. It took some time and a lot of therapy to get here, and I'm still a work in progress. It's hard to love yourself in a world filled with so many celebrities and influencers setting unrealistic standards. Nose jobs, butt implants, lip fillers—you name it, they've done it. So many women feel pressured to change themselves to fit in because social media portrays beauty as one-size-fits-all. *Shame.*

But not me. I will age gracefully and embrace my natural beauty, flaws, stretch marks, and all. Beauty comes in all shapes, sizes, and ages, and I choose to love myself just the way I am. However, it did take me some time to get to this point.

I'm a successful wedding planner who helps brides feel beautiful on their special day, and I love what I do. Have you ever dreamed of the perfect career? I did, and now I'm living it.

It's the best feeling in the world! Of course, there were challenges and obstacles along the way, especially being a Black woman in a predominantly white industry.

There are 10.5 percent Black women in this business, so I had to work twice as hard. My father did it, and I knew I could too.

My father achieved success, while my lazy ass mother didn't do much but got pregnant by a hard-working man. Life was handed to her on a silver platter. She has never worked a day in her life, and she wants the same for me.

Because I reject being a "stay-at-home parent" like her, she undermines my accomplishments and labels me as a washed-up thirty-something who will never find a husband. The only good thing she has given me is a fantastic father. Don't get me wrong, there's nothing wrong with being a stay-at-home parent; however, that lifestyle isn't for me, and she doesn't understand that. You could say my mother isn't my favorite parent of the two.

Oh! I forgot to mention that today is my birthday. I am thirty-three years old, and much to my mother's dismay, I am still unmarried and have no children. My little sister, Skylar, is the golden child in my mother's eyes. She is spoiled rotten and has never had to lift a finger for anything, but I love her—she is more genuine when she isn't being influenced by our mother, bitchy cousins, or her friend, Darcy. Skylar works as my co-event planner at my small boutique, where we plan weddings for fifteen to twenty couples each spring and summer. In the fall and winter seasons, I have about ten to fifteen couples. My long-term goal is to broaden the scope of my business. This means that in addition to wedding planning, I will also venture into organizing different types of events.

Skylar did not interview for that position. My mother, who does not own an ounce of my small business, gave it to her.

She is fine with Skylar working at my boutique but not with me pursuing my career.

Make it make sense.

Switching on the light in my walk-in closet, I glide my fingers over the neatly hung rows of pencil skirts and blouses, determining what to wear. After careful consideration, I've decided on a dark violet off-the-shoulder bodycon dress since I'm going to a bar with my friends and sister for drinks after work.

Before heading to the bathroom, I carefully lay the dress on my king-size bed and reach into my jewelry box for my favorite specialized gold bracelet with a black rose charm.

After my shower, I tuck my black and honey blonde box braids into a bun, apply makeup, and slip into my dress. New York City is always bustling, so I request an Uber. I rarely drive in the city, preferring to avoid the stress of finding parking.

My job is about a forty-five-minute commute, but I don't mind the distance. I'm currently negotiating with a bride who wants a princess-themed wedding and another who wants a Valentine's Day-themed wedding in June. Yeah, a Valentine's Day-themed wedding in June, but who am I to judge?

Once there, I walk through the doors of my small boutique. The bell above the door chimes, and Nancy looks up from behind the counter with a smile.

"Good morning, Nancy," I greet her, making my way to the back of the store to my office.

The display of princess crowns I purchased from my favorite wedding shop in Farmingdale catches my eye, and I smile as I remember the excitement of finding them.

If I ever get married, I will buy my dress from there.

They give me a small discount on all items I purchase from their store, and they love that I always recommend them to my brides.

One day, I hope to sell wedding dresses in my boutique, but for the time being, I only offer bridal accessories. I have a variety of elegant clutch bags, artificial flower bouquets, and beautiful jewelry, along with a list of carefully chosen venue options and limousine suggestions for my clients.

I place my jacket on the coat hanger and hang my purse beside it. Lowering myself into my chair, I scroll through my emails and check my schedule for the day.

I have a bridal appointment in twenty minutes.

"Ms. Brown, your four o'clock canceled, and would like to reschedule for tomorrow," Nancy informs me, walking into my office.

Looking away from my computer screen, I reply, "I will be out of the office tomorrow. Please pencil her in for Friday at the same time."

Nancy furrows her eyebrows as she frantically scans her clipboard, her long auburn hair gently brushing against her shoulders. "Am I missing something?" She mumbles to herself, and then her eyes widen in realization. "I am so sorry, Ms. Brown. I didn't realize today was your birthday! Happy birthday! Why didn't you clear your schedule today?"

I thank her for the birthday wishes with a warm smile. "It's okay, Nancy. I love what I do, and I don't mind working on my birthday. Plus, I only had two meetings scheduled for today, and now that one of them has been rescheduled, I can wrap up my meeting with Ms. Robertson and leave early."

She nods with relief as her eyes light up. "That's wonderful, Ms. Brown! I hope you have a fantastic birthday!"

My phone rings, and I see that it's Skylar.

"Thank you, Nancy. I really appreciate it," I say, wrapping up my conversation with her before answering Skylar's call. She informs me that Ms. Robertson is here and ready for our meeting.

"I'm sure you will secure this client," Nancy says, giving me two thumbs up.

Putting on my best game face, I grab my bridal binder of wedding ideas from the top drawer, determined to impress the bride-to-be with my proposal and convince her I am the perfect fit to plan her dream wedding.

Chapter 2: Reign

Skylar opens the door to my office, allowing Ms. Robertson to enter, her bright red stiletto heels clicking against the floor as she walks. Ms. Robertson's presence fills the room with a sense of elegance and determination. Skylar nods as she closes the door behind my potential client.

Standing to my feet, I offer her a kind smile. "Hello, Ms. Robertson. It's nice to see you again. Please, have a seat." I greet, gesturing toward the chair. Feeling a sense of urgency, I waste no time sliding under my desk, the screeching sound of my chair echoing through the room.

Ms. Robertson takes a seat across from me, gracefully crossing her legs and placing her black and red purse on her lap. She is deep in thought, her distant gaze suggesting the burden of planning for her wedding.

Hopefully, my ideas will alleviate some of that stress. I've seen firsthand how wedding planning can put a strain on brides, with many experiencing emotional breakdowns from the overwhelming pressure.

"Are you ready to begin?"

She focuses on her phone, responding with a slight nod. *Hmm…that's odd.* She's acting a little strange since our last meeting, but I shrug it off as nerves and open my binder.

"So, you're planning a princess-themed wedding; here are some dress options from the questionnaire you completed last week." I flip through the pages. I have four dresses in mind that I think she will love.

She leans forward, scanning the dresses with a furrowed brow. "Why are we looking at dresses before deciding on a venue or decorations?"

I clasp my hands together. "Well, the dress often sets the tone for the wedding, so I like to start there and then move on to other details like the venue and decorations."

She nods slowly, still looking uncertain.

"Once we find the perfect dress, everything else will fall into place."

She still appears uninterested as I show her the first dress again. It's an off-the-shoulder princess ballgown with a tulle lace chapel train.

She bites her bottom lip, not entirely convinced. "It's okay, but it's not for me."

My shoulders droop slightly. "That's completely fine," I say with a polite smile.

Although I had shoes, a veil, and a tiara in mind that would complement the dress perfectly.

"Let's keep looking." I flip to the next page. "What about this one?" I suggest, pointing to the second dress.

It's a scoop neck princess ballgown with a tulle lace sweep train, and before she can give her opinion, I show her the matching accessories I had in mind.

"This dress goes with the pearl rhinestone leaf headband," I suggest, hoping to see her face light up with excitement, but she isn't as enthusiastic as I had hoped.

Clearing my throat, I add, "A scoop neckline will highlight your collarbone beautifully. As you mentioned, you prefer a dress that covers your back. The buttons down the back add elegance and coverage. It also has a built-in bra for support."

She brushes her loose curls away from her face, bored with my suggestions. "Reign, I really don't think this is the dress for me. I'm not sure you're going in the right direction with what I'm looking for."

Taken aback by her response, I pause and consider her feedback. "I appreciate your honesty, Ms. Robertson. I have selected two other options that I think you may like better. Or we can find some other choices that align with what you're looking for in a dress."

"No, that won't be necessary. What decor suggestions do you have in mind?"

"I think you should at least take a look at the other two dresses."

She stands to leave, but I stop her. "Just take a quick look, and if you still don't like them, we can move on to discussing decorations," I compromise.

She rolls her eyes. "I don't want to waste my time looking at dresses I already know I won't like!"

Bitch!

Swallowing my frustration, I nod and flip to the decorations tab in my binder. "Of course."

The dress is the first thing I like to decide on with my clients. Other wedding planners may have different approaches, but I find that choosing the dress is an important starting point for setting the ambiance of the entire wedding. It can help guide decisions about decorations, venue, and even the overall color scheme. Forcing a smile, I shift the conversation to decorations. However, before I can delve into the specifics, Ms. Robertson stands abruptly to leave.

"I don't think you are the right fit for me. You lack the competence I am looking for in a wedding planner."

A pang of disappointment washes over me, yet I remain professional. "Ms. Robertson, my decision-making is based on the questionnaire you filled out at our initial consultation."

Before creating a bridal binder, every bride is required to answer an extensive questionnaire that guides the planning process. There are all sorts of questions about personal style, budget constraints, preferred themes, and specific visions for the wedding.

"Well, you didn't capture my vision. I would rather work with someone who understands my needs." She eyes me warily before continuing. "Which clearly isn't you."

She wanted a long-sleeved lace ballgown with a train. What's not to understand?

"Good day," she says curtly, hastening out of my office before I could respond.

With a frown, I watch her retreating figure disappear into the distance. *What a bitch!* I think to myself, tossing the binder I worked hard on for hours into the trash. I am very competent at what I do; she can find someone else to work with. It's okay; my services are not for everyone, and that's fine. Still, I need another client for this season.

Sighing in defeat, I grab my coat and purse, my mind still reeling from the encounter with Ms. Robertson, and head out the door.

Nancy meets me in the hallway, offering a sympathetic smile. "I'm sorry, we didn't book her. I overheard her on the phone talking about how she found someone cheaper."

Gritting my teeth, I mutter, "I wish I didn't waste my time putting together her binder!" Taking a deep breath and exhaling, "I don't have to book every client."

Ms. Robertson could have just said she found someone cheaper instead of insulting me.

"That's the spirit! Enjoy the rest of your birthday!" Nancy says, nudging me with her elbow.

A feeble smile escapes my lips. "Thank you, Nancy."

And with that, I turn on my heel and head outside to hail a taxi.

I'm the first to show up at the bar for drinks. My friends are always late, and I'll probably still be nursing my first drink by the time they arrive.

The bartender approaches me with a sexy smile. "What can I get you started with?"

"I'll take a Long Island Iced Tea, please."

He chuckles and says, "Coming right up."

My brows knit together. "What's so funny?"

He shakes his head, still grinning. "Nothing, nothing. A Long Island Iced Tea packs a punch, that's all." He says, balling up his fist.

I relax my expression and smile back at him. "It's been a

day, and it's my birthday. I could use it."

He nods his head. "Well then, happy birthday. I'll make sure it's extra strong for you."

As he turns to prepare my drink, August is walking over to the bar. *Oh! She's early for a change.*

"Hey, girl!" She greets me with a hug and a big smile. "Happy birthday!" She brushes her dark brown curly hair to the side and sits next to me, her short legs swaying back and forth on the bar stool.

August is my only happily married friend. She married her college sweetheart Calvin, and they've been in the honeymoon phase ever since. They're so happy; it's almost unreal. They've been together for over ten years, and they're still not bored with each other. How can someone have sex with the same person for that long without getting tired of it? All I have is Rocky, my trusty vibrator. Don't judge me! Rocky never disappoints me, and he always hits the right spot, unlike the men I've been with.

"Girl, are you here or in la-la land?" August teases, her long eyelashes fluttering as she smirks. She tucks a loose curl behind her ear, and the soft light dances across her glowing brown skin.

Shaking my head, I snap out of my thoughts and chuckle, "Sorry, just lost in my own little world for a moment."

August raises an eyebrow, her playful expression turning into a deliberate smile. "I think I know exactly what world you were in," she says with a wink, causing me to nudge her shoulder.

"How was work today?" I ask, changing the subject.

August is the proud owner of a highly regarded cleaning service and is known throughout the city for her exceptional attention to detail. However, the high demand for her services sometimes leaves her feeling stressed and overwhelmed. In order to meet the growing demand, she needs to hire additional workers.

August sighs, her smile fading slightly. "Same old, same old." She shifts her weight on the stool. "How about you? Did you snag the princess client you wanted so badly?"

Rolling my eyes, I let out an exaggerated sigh. "No, and I have no idea why." I lie through my teeth.

"She found someone cheaper instead," Skylar says, joining the conversation with Darcy.

August gives me a smirk and shakes her head, knowing I told a blatant lie.

"Hi, ladies!" Darcy chirps, twirling her blonde hair around her finger. "What are we talking about?" She asks, looking between Skylar and me. She always wants to insert herself into everything.

"Wedding planning drama," Skylar explains, filling Darcy in on the situation with the princess client while I ignore Darcy and raise an eyebrow at Skylar.

"Wait, how do you know that?"

"I may have overheard her talking on the phone," Skylar admits nonchalantly.

"You mean to tell me both you and Nancy overheard her? Why didn't you mention it earlier?"

She shrugs her shoulders. "I didn't think it was important at the time."

"Here is your drink," the bartender says, interrupting our conversation. "Are you sure you can handle it?"

I raise an eyebrow, a challenge in my eyes. "Try me."

The ladies start howling at our interaction, and my cheeks

begin to flush.

He winks at me before turning back to the bar.

"He was giving you sexy eyes," August teases, nudging me with her elbow.

Taking a sip of my drink and internally gagging, I roll my eyes playfully at her comment. He didn't lie when he said he would make it strong.

"*Hola,* ladies!" Scarlette shouts as she joins our group, her eyes glued to her phone as usual. "Happy birthday, *mi amor,*" she says, wrapping me in a tight hug. When we break apart, she leans against the bar, standing on her tippy toes and fluttering her hazel eyes to get the bartender's attention. "Can you bring us a round of tequila shots, *por favor? Muchas gracias.*"

The bartender winks and prepares the shots for us.

Scarlette, infamously known as "Escarletta Lucia Rodriguez," is my spicy Latina and over-the-top best friend. She loves to be the center of attention and always knows how to bring the party wherever she goes. We have been friends since pre-school, and she is my partner in crime for life.

"Here's to the amazing Reign; happy birthday!" Scarlette exclaims, recording the moment on her phone. "*¡Salud!*" She raises her shot glass, clinking it against ours, and downs the tequila in one swift motion.

When the tequila hits my tongue, my taste buds awaken, and a burning sensation spreads through my body. I suppress a cough and welcome it with a smile.

"Let's get a table," Darcy suggests.

We nod, following her lead to a table in the corner of the crowded bar.

"I have some exciting news to share with you guys!" Skylar

announces when we are all seated.

We look at her expectantly, waiting for her to spill the beans.

She squeals, flashing the sparkling diamond ring on her finger with a massive grin spreading across her face. *What? I didn't notice her ring earlier.* She and Peter haven't been dating for that long. A rush of foreign emotions floods through me as I process her unexpected news. Howling erupts from our group as they gather around Skylar to congratulate her on her engagement.

Trying to wrap my head around the fact that my little sister is getting married before me, I sit there in stunned silence. My mother is going to throw this in my face for the rest of my life. Scarlette nudges me with her elbow, a knowing look in her eyes. This is Skylar's moment, and I should be happy for her.

Forcing a smile, I join in the celebration. "Congratulations, sis! I'm so happy for you," I say, hugging her tight.

"Thank you! I still can't believe it myself." Skylar beams with excitement and gushes, "He proposed on our anniversary. It was so romantic!"

Anniversary for what? *Three minutes?* They haven't even been together for an entire year.

The girls gather around to admire her engagement ring as I stare off into the distance and sip my drink.

Feeling a pang of jealousy creeping in, I wonder: What, why, and how? My twenty-four-year-old sister is engaged. I never cared much about marriage before, but seeing Skylar so happy and in love makes me question if I'm missing out on something special. I don't know what I was expecting; however, I was not expecting Skylar to be the first of us two.

"Reign, are you okay?" August asks, noticing my distant

expression.

I snap out of my thoughts and force a smile. "Yeah, I'm fine. Just daydreaming again."

Scarlette eyes me warily. "Are you sure? You seem a little distant."

"Where did Sky and Darcy go?" I ask, realizing they are no longer at the table.

"Girl, they left. You said bye to them, don't you remember?" August chuckles.

Feeling embarrassed, I shake my head.

Scarlette pats my shoulder. "No more Long Island Iced Tea's for you, Reign."

August leans in, giggling. "I can't believe she's marrying Peter Peterson. Who names their child that?"

We share a knowing look and burst into laughter.

"It's like a bad joke," I add, still chuckling.

"Peter. Pete-er-son," Scarlette repeats, emphasizing each syllable. "Why did they do him like that?"

We laugh until our stomachs hurt.

"Poor Peter Peterson," I say between giggles.

Scarlette shakes her head, knotting her light brown hair into a messy bun. "He must have a solid ego to survive that name."

I snort in agreement.

August's phone rings, and her face lights up.

Scarlette and I exchange a glance. Hubby is calling.

"I'll see you guys later. My honey dip is outside."

Once August is out of sight, Scarlette turns to me with a severe expression. "Reign, I know you. What's wrong?"

Knowing I can't hide anything from her, I sigh. "I didn't think my baby sister announcing her engagement would bother me so much. It just gives my mother more ammunition to use against me."

"Aw, Reign, *lo siento*," she says, wrapping her arms around me. "Your mom is a total bitch."

"And so are my cousins," I add. "This will be yet another wedding that I attend dateless. Those bitches are going to have a field day over this!"

Scarlette is silent for a moment before pulling back and looking me in the eyes with a mischievous glint. "Unless…"

She can't just start a sentence like that and not finish it. "Unless what?"

"Follow me." She stands from her seat, pulling me up with her.

Furrowing my brows, I follow her to the bathroom, curious about what she has up her sleeve.

She checks each bathroom stall.

"Girl, what are you doing?" I sigh in exasperation.

When she's sure we're alone, she turns to me with a sly smile. "We're going to find you a date for the wedding."

I raise an eyebrow. "And how exactly do you propose we do that?"

"I am currently beta testing a new dating app for my business."

My curiosity piques. "Go on, I'm listening."

Scarlette explains how the app's new feature matches people based on their interests and compatibility, helping them reach a mutual agreement.

"We can hire you a boyfriend."

"You can't be serious?!"

"Absolutely serious. It's completely legit and safe. Look," she says, showing me the app on her phone.

"No, thank you," I spit out, not comfortable with the idea of hiring someone to pretend to be my man. "How pathetic do you think I am?"

Who hires a boyfriend?

Scarlette shrugs, unfazed by my reaction. "It's just a service, like any other. Think of it as a temporary solution to your problem," she suggests. "There are plenty of successful and independent women who don't have time to date but still want companionship. It's becoming more common these days, and I created a safe space for women like you to explore that option without judgment."

Maybe she has a point. Or perhaps I'm just desperate enough to consider it.

Her phone beeping pulls me out of my thoughts.

She looks at me apologetically, and my eyes bug out as she shows me a notification from her dating app.

"Escarletta, what did you do?!"

She holds her hands up in defense. "I may have matched you with someone."

"You did what?!"

"Just give it a chance, Reign," she pleads, batting her eyelashes.

"That was a little too bold, even for you." I let out a sigh, unable to stay mad at her for long. I can at least look at the profile. "How did I get matched so fast?"

Scarlette grins. She always gets what she wants. "This is a beta test, so there are only three candidates, and my algorithm found the perfect match for you, but we can cancel if you're not interested. He didn't accept the match yet, so you still have time to back out."

Scarlette hands me her phone, and I reluctantly start

scrolling through the profile. He looks vaguely familiar, but I can't quite place where I've seen him before. His name is Dion James, and the more I read, the more intrigued I become.

"Wait, is this the same dude from that commercial? You know…what was it again? I think it was for peanut butter?"

Scarlette peeks over my shoulder, her eyes widening. "Oh yeah, that's him! He was every seven-year-old's dream guy!" she jokes, nudging me playfully.

I roll my eyes at her exaggerated reaction and continue scrolling through the profile. "It says he's looking for an acting gig, which would be kind of perfect if I were to go through with this crazy idea."

Scarlette claps her hands together smiling, her eyes wide with excitement.

Biting my bottom lip, I weigh the pros and cons. My mother will finally stop nagging me about finding a boyfriend. Plus, he's hot. *Really hot.* You could get lost in his light brown eyes, and he has a strong and sculpted build that would make any girl swoon. My cousins would definitely be jealous if they saw me with him. He is the perfect candidate for a fake boyfriend. The worst that could happen is real feelings getting involved, but that's not likely. He's an actor, after all; he knows how to fake emotions for a living. And I have always been good at keeping my emotions in check. How hard could it be to pretend to be in love for a little while?

"Okay, I'll do it. How does this work?" I reply, handing the phone back to her.

Scarlette smirks and replies, "How long do you need him for? And how much are you willing to pay for his services?"

How pathetic am I? *UGH.*

Scarlette chuckles when she sees my face. "Just let me

know your terms, and we can make it happen."

"I don't want this to blow up in my face," I mutter, feeling embarrassed by the whole situation. "I just need him until Skylar and Peter get married…" I trail off. "Whenever that is."

Scarlette narrows her eyes at me.

"What?"

"They are getting married in October, Reign. She literally just told you that not too long ago." She shakes her head, clearly amused.

"I totally tuned out after Sky said she was getting married," I admit sheepishly.

Scarlette laughs. "I can't with you sometimes," she says before turning serious again. "You have three options: One month, four months, or six. Which time frame works best for you?"

I do the math in my head and blurt out, "Six months should be perfect."

"Six months is ten thousand dollars," Scarlette informs me. She tilts her head to the side. "Are you sure you want to commit to that?"

Taken aback by the price, I pause for a moment. "I really don't want to be the pun of every joke at Sky's wedding, so I guess I'll have to make it work somehow."

There are moments like these when my confidence wavers. While I take pride in my strength and independence as a single woman, I can't help but wish for a date to accompany me to my baby sister's wedding.

Scarlette nods, typing into her phone. "I scheduled a meet and greet for tomorrow so you can discuss the details with him."

"Oh shit, that was fast!"

"That's the beauty of technology, baby," she says with a wink. "Now, let's head back to the dance floor and enjoy the rest of your birthday."

My mind is still reeling from the sudden turn of events as I follow her lead. I'm either making the best decision of my life or setting myself up for a disaster.

Only time will tell.

Chapter 3: Dion

Fidgeting in my seat, I wait for my name to be called to audition for a commercial, which will hopefully lead to another opportunity and a larger role—perhaps in a movie. I've enjoyed acting since I was eight years old, but I've found staying relevant in this competitive industry to be a constant challenge. You are only as good as your next best character, and I haven't played a significant role in over five years. I did land a recurring role on a teen drama sitcom called "The Richards" until they gradually phased me out for someone younger and more attractive.

I started in this industry as *the* Dion Atom James—a child star on the rise, ready to take over the world; now I'm sitting here hoping to land an underwear commercial.

An attractive young woman walks to the front of the room, sighing heavily as she carries a brown clipboard. "Mr. James? You are up next."

Taking a moment to adjust my posture, I stand up with confidence and wear a sexy grin on my face. "That's me."

Her eyes scan me up and down, and I flex my muscles instinctively to charm her. The woman notices, and her almond skin turns a faint pink. Oh yeah! I've still got it.

"Follow me," she says with a slight smile, leading me to the audition room and swaying her hips as she walks.

Walking confidently behind her, I mentally prepare myself for this audition. We stop in front of a black door with a gold star.

She turns to me with a smile and wishes me, "Good luck."

I flash her another winning grin before taking a deep breath as she pushes open the door. When I step inside, the nerves start to kick in. The room feels cold and empty, and there's no one in sight. I pull out my phone to text my agent, confirming that I'm in the right place. I've heard of shady places like this before, preying on aspiring actors and models looking for their big break. My agent immediately responds that I am indeed in the correct location and that this is legit.

"Mr. James," a stern voice calls out from behind me.

Turning around, I see that it's none other than Taycole Buckland, the famous designer known for her innovative approach to underwear in New York, accompanied by two assistants. *Wow!*

She looks me up and down before extending her hand and introducing herself.

"N–nice to meet you," I stammer, feeling starstruck and shaking her hand like a maniac. *Get it together, James.*

"It's nice to meet you too," she says before quickly pulling her hand away like she had contracted a deadly disease from me.

Taycole offers her hand to the man standing beside her, and he swiftly retrieves a bottle of hand sanitizer from his pocket and squeezes it into her hand.

"Please change into this underwear for the fitting. We will take some photos of you, and then we will give you your lines," the woman next to Taycole says, handing me a pair of black briefs.

Looking at the underwear, it doesn't seem like there is enough room for my package, but I nod and take it, heading towards the dressing room. Their wary gazes follow me, their silent judgment searing into my back as I walk away. I hastily change out of my clothes and into the underwear provided. They are too small, but what am I supposed to do? I step out of the dressing room, catching the woman next to Taycole turning bright red at the sight of me while the man awkwardly averts his gaze. Taycole Buckland herself raises an eyebrow, and I cover my bulge with my hands while trying to suppress a smirk.

"Please stand over there so we can take some photos," she says, gesturing towards the backdrop.

"Maybe we should have given him a larger size," the woman suggests quietly to Taycole.

She's not wrong; this size is way too small for me.

The photographer is kneeling, adjusting his camera settings as I walk toward the backdrop. When he's finished, our gaze meets.

He clears his throat. "I'm ready when you are."

I remove my hands from my bulge and strike a few poses as the camera clicks away. The photographer seems satisfied with the shots. "Yes, yes, just like that, perfect! You're a natural in front of the camera!"

Taycole and her two assistants watch from the sidelines, exchanging whispers with each other.

As the photographer wraps up the shoot, I stop posing. He flicks through the photos on his camera and nods in approval. "I think I have enough."

Taycole approaches me, handing me a script to rehearse, and the photographer packs up his equipment. "You have fifteen minutes to memorize your lines before we start filming."

I take the script from her and start going over my lines.

Comfortable fit?

Yes.

Perfect for any package.

Are you kidding me? I tug at the band of my underwear that's digging into my skin. The longer I wear them, the more uncomfortable they become.

These briefs are not the perfect fit for larger packages because my balls are suffocating in them! *This industry!*

Fifteen Minutes Later...

"Are you ready?" The young woman behind the camera asks me.

I nod in response and step in front of the camera. *Lights, camera, action!* The filming begins, and I deliver my lines effortlessly over and over again until the director is satisfied with the take. The young woman gives me a thumbs up. *I nailed it!*

"That's a wrap for today." The woman says.

Hurrying to the dressing room, I've never been so eager to strip down when there's no sex involved until now.

On my way out the door, a beautiful woman stops me and says her team will be in touch. With a wink, she slips her phone number into my pocket.

I take the train back to Long Island and go to my one-bedroom apartment to shower and change. I need to be quick because I'm already twenty minutes late for lunch with my parents. Every Wednesday has become a special tradition for us since my mom beat breast cancer. We have lunch together to commemorate another week of her being in remission.

When I was in sixth grade, my mother was diagnosed with stage three cancer because of the size of the tumor in her breast. Surgery was her first line of defense, followed by chemo and eight weeks of radiation treatments. After the eight weeks, she continued to take cancer treatment pills for five years. She's been cancer-free for twenty-four years, and I can't thank God enough for saving her life.

I arrive at the restaurant and see her sitting at our usual table. However, my dad is nowhere in sight.

I kiss her on the forehead, and she lightly scolds me for being late. "I've already ordered our meals, Atom."

My middle name is Atom, which is pronounced *Adam* but spelled differently because my mother loved science when she was younger. She was keen on naming me after something related to science. My father preferred a more traditional name, so they compromised with *Atom* as my middle name instead. My parents have been happily married for thirty-seven years now and are retired. They are enjoying this new chapter in their lives by going on vacations and spending time with me.

"I'm sorry, mom. Thank you for ordering for us." I apologize to her for my tardiness. "Will you forgive me?"

She rolls her eyes and responds, "I'll think about it."

I smile, showcasing the dimple on my left cheek. "I promise it won't happen again."

Mom lets out a loud sigh, patting my hand, "You always know how to charm your way out of trouble, Atom."

Another grin forms on my lips and she winks at me.

"Where is Dad?"

"He wasn't feeling well today so he decided to stay back."

"Is he okay?" I ask, a crease forming between my brows.

"Yes, he just needs to rest. How was your day today?"

"It was pretty good. I had an audition today."

She scrunches up her face. "What did you audition for this time?" Her voice is angelic, but you can hear the annoyance in her tone.

My mom disapproves of the showbiz industry. She would prefer that I pursue a more stable career instead. Although I am a single, thirty-four-year-old man living in a shitty apartment with barely enough money to pay rent, I still dream of making it big in this industry one day.

Knowing her reaction would be disapproving, I downplayed the audition and said, "Just a commercial."

Mom narrows her eyes for me to continue. I add sheepishly, "An underwear commercial."

She sucks her teeth and shakes her head, clearly unimpressed.

Steering the conversation away from my career aspirations, I change the subject to her. "How was your day today, Mom?"

She sighs and then starts talking about her day. "It was okay. Your father and I went for our usual walk before he started to feel unwell. We talked about saving some money to take a nice vacation to the Bahamas this summer."

"That's great, mom! Do you need any help paying for the trip?"

My mom gives me a knowing look and replies, "Oh, Atom, you don't have to worry about that. We've got it covered. Perhaps you should focus on getting a *real* job instead."

Before I can respond, the waitress arrives at our booth with our food, interrupting our conversation. *Perfect timing.* I don't want to have this discussion with her yet again.

We thank the waitress and dig into our meals. I always order the double-stacked turkey burger, loaded with pickles, onions, and mushrooms and smothered in BBQ sauce. My mom is conscious of her weight and chooses the Caesar salad. As we enjoy our lunch together, our conversation shifts to lighter topics. After finishing our meal, I offered to pay the bill, but Mom politely declined. She picks up the check, and we leave the restaurant. I kiss her goodbye, and then we part ways.

I head back to my apartment to get ready before meeting my friend at the bar. It might be too early to say, but I believe I may have secured the commercial opportunity.

Eddie and I grab a table when we arrive at the bar in the city. We don't normally come to this bar; however, I wanted a change of scenery. It's busy tonight, but we managed to find a spot in the corner. We walk past a group of beautiful women laughing and chatting, and one of them catches my eye.

She's wearing a stunning purple off-the-shoulder dress that complements her body perfectly, and the black rose charm on her gold bracelet catches the light as she gestures animatedly. *Damn! She's beautiful.* Almost tripping over my own feet, I steal glances at her as we make our way to the table. I haven't been in a serious relationship for about five years. I've had several casual flings, but nothing tangible. Besides, my profession makes it hard for me to commit or provide stability.

We take our seats and order a round of shots. Eddie is my only friend from high school. As time went by, my circle of friends got smaller.

"Did you get that commercial?" he asks.

"I'm waiting to hear back from my agent," I reply, trying to sound nonchalant. "It would be a big break for me if I did."

Eddie nods, knowing how hard I've been working to make it in the industry. "How long does it usually take for them to get back to you?"

I shrug and say, "Sometimes she gets back to me within a few days, and other times it can take weeks. But since I was the last one to audition, I shouldn't have to wait too long before I hear something."

The bartender arrives with our shots, and we raise them high.

"Eddie chuckles and asks, "What are we toasting to this time?"

"To being alive!" I toast, and we chug our shots in one gulp.

My phone rings as I set down the empty shot glass. "Speak of the devil," I say, glancing at the screen. "It's my agent."

"Better answer that," Eddie says with a grin.

Hoping for good news, I answer the call.

Me: "Hello?"

Agent: "Hello Dion, I have some bad news. The casting director decided to go with someone else. Maybe next time."

My shoulders slump.

Me: "Thanks for letting me know."

Agent: "I'll keep looking for other opportunities for you. However, I expect to receive your payment by next week."

Me: "I'll have it to you by then."

I hang up the phone, disappointment written all over my face. I used the money I had to pay my rent for this month.

Eddie knows my expression all too well. "Bro, do you need to borrow some money again?"

Not wanting to rely on him yet again, I shake my head. "Nah, I got it. I'll figure something out."

"You sure?"

"Yeah, I'll make it work somehow," I assure him, trying to sound more confident than I feel.

I think about how much money I have in my bank account, and it's a joke. But I can't keep taking cash from Eddie every time I'm in a bind. He works as a bank teller. I used to make fun of him for it because he wanted to be a model, but he gave up on that dream a long time ago.

Eddie looks at his phone, glancing between me and the screen.

"What is it?" I ask, a sense of dread creeping in.

He bursts into laughter and says, "I downloaded a dating app called *Scarletta*. Check this out—there is an opening for a *Fake Boyfriend* listed. I think I found your next job opportunity!"

It takes a few seconds for the *fake boyfriend* thing to catch me. "Very funny, Eddie."

"Bro, I'm serious," he insists, showing me the listing on his phone. "You could make some easy money pretending to be someone's boyfriend."

Raising an eyebrow, I consider the idea. "I don't know. It sounds kind of sketchy."

Eddie shrugs. "It's just acting, right? Plus, it's not like you have to commit to anything long-term."

"True," I reply, still unsure. "But what if the person catches feelings or something?"

Eddie chuckles. "That's their problem, not yours. Just think of it as a side hustle."

"I guess it couldn't hurt to give it a try," I say, finally agreeing.

Eddie grins, already typing out a response to the listing and creating a profile for me. He nods towards the back of the bar, and I follow him outside to discuss the app.

"A woman you were matched with requested a meet and greet tomorrow. Are you up for it?"

"Oh shit, that was fast!"

Eddie laughs. "It looks like you're in demand already."

"How pathetic is this woman to hire someone to pretend to be her boyfriend?"

He shrugs. "Who knows, but she's offering a couple thousand for six months of pretending!"

"Woah! Seriously?!"

"Yeah, bro. You've hit the jackpot with this acting gig!" Eddie claps me on the back. "It looks like you'll be rolling in cash soon."

Thank you, God! This is a blessing in disguise.

"Accept her offer," I say as Eddie taps his phone to confirm the meet-and-greet.

Just when my back is against the wall, God comes through for me.

Chapter 4: Reign

Scarlette and I hail a taxi to meet Dion James and his friend at Central Park. We agreed that meeting in a public place would be the best option. Central Park and Wollman Rink are two of my favorite spots to go to and will forever hold a special place in my heart. A smile spreads across my face as I reminisce about when I was younger. The day after one of my games, Scarlette and her family would often whisk me away to Central Park or Wollman Rink as a way to celebrate. And sometimes, when my dad couldn't make it to a game, he would join us right before heading to work.

We get into the taxi, and Scarlette's face lights up with a huge grin.

"What are you so smiley-smiley about?" I ask.

"Because you are about to meet your man!" she says, wriggling her eyebrows.

"My 'fake' man, you mean." I correct her, gesturing air quotes around the word *fake*.

Scarlette nudges me playfully and says, "Same difference."

I roll my eyes and lean my head against the window while Scarlette busies herself with her phone. Staring out the window, I think back to my last relationship. His name was Max, and the beginning was exhilarating. The sex was good, full of excitement and promise. But as time went on, the cracks began to show, and it was his infidelities that made me realize he wasn't the one for me. We ended on less than pleasant terms, and I haven't dived back into the dating pool since then—it's been roughly seven years. That jerk is a friend of the family, so I occasionally see him at gatherings, and despite his cheating, my mother still loves him.

Old wounds start to resurface, causing my heart to kick into high gear, pounding against my chest and sending adrenaline rushing through my veins. The air in the taxi suddenly feels heavy. I roll down the window, trying to catch my breath. Scarlette is glued to her phone, so she doesn't notice my distress. *Thank God.*

I focus on the passing scenery outside while memories come flooding back. During the early summer, when I was working at a Bridal shop, I found myself juggling the wedding and prom seasons simultaneously. As a result, private sessions with clients often became overwhelming, leaving little time for breaks. However, amidst the chaos, I managed to squeeze in a visit to Max's apartment for a quick nap in between meetings. Little did I know what awaited me behind his closed door one fateful afternoon. He had a bitch bent over his bed, relentlessly pounding into her. When he finally noticed me standing in the doorway, he finished inside her, and I left without saying a word. He didn't follow me out right away; I guess he wanted to wrap things up with his bitch before chasing after me. I ghosted him after that. My heart was shattered, and I swore off men, making the conscious decision to center my focus on myself and my career instead. With my sister's wedding coming up, the pressure of finding a partner and starting a family is gnawing at me now. Once Skylar's wedding is over, I suppose I'll start putting myself out there again.

Lost in my thoughts, I failed to notice the familiar scent of freshly cut grass and the sound of children and adults laughing as we arrived at the entrance of Central Park. The lush greenery and sounds of nature instantly lift my spirits. Scarlette and I walk towards the bridge overlooking the serene lake. We're early, so I take a moment to breathe in the fresh air. As I inhale, my stomach knots with nerves at meeting Dion for the first time. I lean over the railing, watching the ducks swim by in an attempt to calm my racing heart. The gentle breeze brushes against my skin, carrying away some of my anxiety. I've caught glimpses of him on a few shows in the past, but it seems like he hasn't been in anything recent, indicating that he might not be pursuing acting roles right now. Or perhaps I have been too preoccupied with my career.

Scarlette nudges me with her elbow. "There he is," she whispers, pointing towards two figures approaching us from the other side of the bridge. As Dion's familiar face comes into view, a rush of excitement washes over me.

As our eyes meet, his warm smile illuminates his brown eyes, giving them a sun-kissed honey-like glow.

"Hi, Reign, is it?" He extends his hand when he reaches us, his voice smooth and inviting.

I get lost in his gaze for a moment, but Scarlette nudges me again, snapping me out of my daze. Trying to keep my cool despite the nerves bubbling in my stomach, I shake his hand with a smile forming on my face. "Yes, that's me."

Flutters of attraction stir inside me, making me feel a connection that I hadn't expected.

Dion's lips curl into a charming grin. "It's nice to meet you in person." His touch lingers on my hand for a moment longer than necessary, igniting a spark of desire that I can't ignore. Fake dating him might be more complicated than I thought.

Scarlette clears her throat. *"Tú estás babeando,"* she scolds me.

The man next to Dion chuckles, and I quickly pull my hand away from Dion, exchanging an eye roll with Scarlette. His friend definitely understood her telling me I was drooling in Spanish.

Dion raises an eyebrow, amused by the interaction. "It's nice to meet you too," he says to Scarlette, flashing a knowing smile at her. "I guess you're the one who organized this meeting."

She smiles. "Yes, I'm Scarlette. My app is growing, and we're testing the fake dating feature before the full launch. I am slowly rolling it out to each of my clients, and you were the first to bite at our listing on the app, so congratulations on being our guinea pig."

The man next to Dion laughs again, and Dion nudges him with his elbow and says, "Eddie here downloaded the app for himself and convinced me to give it a try when he received a notification about the fake dating feature."

Scarlette smiles at Eddie, and he grins back. "Have you had any luck finding a date on my app?"

Eddie chuckles and responds, "Not yet, but I'm hopeful."

She nods, gesturing for her and Eddie to walk further down the bridge to continue their conversation, allowing Dion and me to have some privacy.

As they walk away, I nod towards the grass and suggest, "Let's sit over there on the grass."

Dion agrees, and we walk together, finding a quiet spot to sit and talk. I take out a blanket from my bag and spread it on the grass, patting the spot next to me for him to join me. As we settle in, I pull out a clipboard with my game face on, and his eyes widen.

"What's that for?"

"I have a few things to go over with you to ensure we are a good fit."

He gives me a strange look but then agrees. "Okay, shoot."

Reading through my list, I start firing off questions. "Why do you want this position?"

I note that his shoulders tense slightly before he answers, "I am between jobs right now, and I think this opportunity sounds promising until I find something more permanent."

"What do you mean by that?"

Dion scratches his head. "Which part?"

"What do you mean by you're between jobs?"

"I'm an actor, so I'm currently looking for my next role. It's been a little difficult finding work lately, so I'm exploring other options in the meantime."

"Oh? I had no idea you're an actor." I lie, pretending I don't know who he is.

A crease forms between his eyebrows as he studies me. "Yes, I did a few commercials. I'm sure you've seen me in something before. I also mentioned it on my profile."

I shake my head, playing dumb. "Hmm...I may have missed

that because it's not ringing any bells."

He narrows his eyes at me. "Well, hopefully, I'll land a big role soon, and you won't be able to miss me."

Blushing slightly, I quickly move on to my next question. "When were you last tested for sexually transmitted diseases?"

Dion shifts uncomfortably. "Uh, about a year ago." He pauses before adding, "There is no sex involved in this arrangement. Correct?"

A year?

I nod, trying to keep my expression neutral. "Absolutely no sex. We may have to kiss, but that's as far as it goes, and I don't want to catch herpes or anything else from you."

"Is that right?" Dion chuckles nervously and asks, "When was the last time you were tested?"

I'm the one asking the questions here.

"I get tested often," I reply, and his brows snap together. Retrieving a card from my bag, I hand it to him. "I set up an appointment for you tomorrow to get tested, just to be safe."

His eyes are wide as he takes the card.

"Our next discussion is payment," I state firmly, and he listens as I outline the terms. "I need you to pretend to be my boyfriend for the next six months. In total, I will write you a check for ten thousand dollars: one thousand dollars for the first and last month and two thousand for the rest of the months. Do you agree to these terms?"

He nods slowly, processing the offer. "So, we just need to kiss in public sometimes and go to a few events together."

"That's correct. It's a simple arrangement, just for appearances," I clarify.

Dion visibly relaxes and responds, "Okay, I agree."

"Great! Do you have any questions for me?"

"Two questions, actually," he begins. "First, what do you do for a living that you can afford to pay me ten thousand dollars? And second, why do you need a fake boyfriend? I'm sure an attractive woman such as yourself would have men lining up to date you."

Feeling a little faint at his directness, I blush. "I'm a wedding planner, and my business is doing well. As for why I need a fake boyfriend, I don't have time to date. But my family, especially my mother and cousins, are assholes, and I don't want to attend another wedding single."

"Fair enough," he says, nodding in understanding. "Whose wedding is it?"

"It's my little sister's wedding. She's getting married in October."

"Ah, family pressure," he says with a sympathetic look.

"To make it seem believable, you'll have to play the part of my boyfriend convincingly. My family is *always* in my business."

"Not a problem. I'm a great actor," he replies with a charming smile.

My cheeks flush. "Let's shake on it then," I say, extending my hand for a handshake.

"Deal," he says, shaking my hand firmly. "I'll be the best fake boyfriend you've ever had." He looks at me with recognition in his eyes. "Are you sure we haven't met before? You look familiar."

Trying to brush off the strange feeling his words give me, I shake my head. "I don't think so. Maybe I just have one of those faces."

He chuckles and says, "Maybe."

I can't help but smile back at him, and we continue getting to know each other better.

Chapter 5: Dion

I watch closely as Reign meticulously scans her checklist, her fingers tracing each item with purpose. Despite this being an acting gig, I can't help but admire how lovely her brown skin shines in the sunlight. Her light brown eyes are sparkling, and her body is so fucking sexy. *Damn!* The way she carries herself is a complete turn-on and my manhood notices.

Suddenly, it clicked in my mind—I had seen this woman before! She was the woman in the purple off-the-shoulder dress at the bar with Scarlette last night. It seems like my realization is evident on my face because, as Reign glances up from her checklist, a slight crease appears between her eyebrows. It amazes me that a woman as stunning as she remains single. Is it too personal to ask her that? Her career can't be the only reason she's single, right?

"Is there something you want to ask me?"

"Has your sister set a date for the wedding yet?" I blurt out instead.

"Not yet," she replies. "I'll keep you posted on the date. I will also update you on upcoming events and what you should wear to each."

Nodding my head, I try my best to maintain a neutral expression; however, Reign looks at me as if I had a different question in mind.

"Is there something else you want to ask me?" Reign asks, tilting her head to the side. "The concept of this meet-and-greet is to establish boundaries on what to expect from each other," she adds, her eyes searching mine.

Here goes nothing. "I don't mean to overstep, but is your career the only reason you're single? Or is there more to it?"

She looks taken aback for a moment and slightly annoyed by my question. "My personal life is just that—personal," she responds curtly. "But to answer your question, no, my career is not the only reason I'm single. There are other factors at play that I'd rather not discuss."

I hold up my hand in protest. "I apologize if I crossed a line. If this relationship is to come off as authentic, we should know some personal things about each other. What if someone approaches me at an event and asks about you?"

"I doubt they will ask you why I'm single," she retorts.

That's true; she is hiring me to be her boyfriend, so why would anyone ask why she is single?

"Fair point," I concede. "How about I start by telling you why I'm single instead?"

She crosses her arms over her chest. "I suppose that's only fair."

"It's not a big deal, really," I say with a shrug. "I've always been focused on my acting career and haven't prioritized dating. I want to secure a reoccurring role on a TV sitcom or soap opera—anything at this point—before I commit to a serious relationship."

Her eyes narrow as she studies me. "What does that have to do with dating?"

I may have just dug myself into a deeper hole; however, one of the most important lessons my mother taught me was the value of honesty. Men typically hide their genuine emotions, making it difficult to gauge their feelings. My mother taught me to be different.

"I don't have much to bring to the table in a relationship right now, so why be in one if I can't give it my all?"

Reign's eyes seem to stretch, scanning me from head to toe.

I chuckle at her scrutiny. "What is it?"

She meets my gaze and starts laughing before saying, "I don't know. Most guys would never admit that. It's refreshing to hear someone be so straightforward."

"I've been taught to be honest and upfront about my feelings."

She raises an eyebrow in interest. "Oh, and who taught you that?"

"My mother. We are very close."

"So, you're a momma's boy, huh?" She laughs, and I grin in response.

"What's wrong with that?"

She shrugs, still smiling. "Nothing at all. It's actually quite endearing."

A warm feeling spreads in my chest at her response.

"Fine, I'll tell you why I'm single," she says, indulging my curiosity. "The last time I was in a relationship was about seven years ago, and it ended pretty badly. I walked in on him cheating on me, and I just couldn't bring myself to trust anyone again after that. I've been focusing on myself and my career since then. Hence the need for a fake boyfriend."

As her lips curl into a wry smile, I can see the pain behind her words. Why would any man cheat on her? There are no valid reasons to cheat; just break up.

"I'm sorry that happened to you."

"Thank you," she replies softly. "Have you cheated on anyone before?"

"No, I could never do that to someone," I reply honestly. There's a slight blush on her cheeks as she looks away. "My parents have been in love since middle school. Neither of them cheated. They are the epitome of Black Love."

She swallows hard before responding, "Dion James, you truly are a different breed."

I burst out laughing. "I'll take that as a compliment."

She smiles. "It is. You're easy to talk to, and I enjoy learning more about you. Maybe fake dating you won't be so bad."

"I'm glad you think so." I reply, chuckling.

Scarlette and Eddie are walking back towards us. Looking at my watch, I notice we've been sitting here for an hour, discussing the terms of our fake relationship and getting to know each other.

We wrap up our conversation and stand from the grass to join them.

"Are you two done here?" Scarlette asks, raising an eyebrow.

"Not quite," Reign replies, glancing at me, and I furrow my brows in confusion. "Give me your phone so I can put my number in."

That was sexy.

"Smooth move," I tease, exchanging phones with a grin.

She rolls her eyes and saves her number before handing it back to me. "I'll have my lawyer draw up the contract for our arrangement by tomorrow. I'll text you when it's ready to sign. We can meet alone for that part."

"Sounds good," I say with a smile, already looking forward to our next meeting.

We say our goodbyes, and once the ladies are out of earshot, Eddie turns to me with a knowing grin. "I can't believe you're actually going through with this."

Nudging his shoulder, I snort. "Are you kidding me? It was your idea."

Eddie laughs, shaking his head. "I didn't think you'd actually do it."

"Me neither."

"What do you think about Reign?"

Reign is intelligent, independent, beautiful, and has a sexy body.

Shrugging my shoulders. "She seems cool."

"Cool? That's it? You must be blind, man. She's smoking hot. They both are." Eddie nudges me playfully. "Even a blind man can see that she is fiinnee. Shit, once you two are done, maybe I can date her for real."

I nudge him back. "Dream on, Eddie. She wants a fake boyfriend because she does not have the time for a real one. Plus, she's way out of your league anyway."

Eddie chuckles. "I'll take my chances, man."

"Good luck with that," I say sarcastically. "What did her friend say in Spanish, by the way? Don't think I didn't notice your facial expression."

He laughs and shrugs. "You know my Spanish is bad."

"Dude, you speak Spanish! Tell me what she said!"

He raises his hands in surrender. "Fine, fine. She said Reign was drooling over you."

"She was?"

Eddie shrugs his shoulders. "Well, that's what her friend said."

A smug grin tugs at my lips. Maybe she was attracted to me as much as I was to her, which might complicate this fake dating thing. Still, I push those thoughts aside and keep my eyes on the prize, which is the ten G's. I need the money for rent and so much more.

Eddie nudges me as we walk out the front gate of Central Park to head to the subway. "How much does she plan to pay you?"

Grinning wide, I reply, "Ten G's for six months."

Eddie whistles low. "Not bad for pretending to be someone's boyfriend. You will have enough money to cover your rent and then some."

"I can purchase the new uniforms for the little league basketball team," I add with a grin.

Eddie grins back, nodding in agreement. "That would be awesome."

Shaking my leg vigorously, I wait for my name to be called at the clinic. I don't know why I'm so nervous. Then again, it's been a while since I've gotten tested. I always use a condom, but there's always a slight worry about what would happen if they came back and told me that I had contracted something.

Condoms are only ninety-eight percent effective, after all.

A nurse appears behind the brown doors and calls my name. I stand up and follow her into the examination room.

We enter room four, and I take a seat on the sterile, paper-covered chair. "What brings you in today, Mr. James?"

"Uh, I'm here for routine STI testing," I respond, scratching the back of my neck nervously.

"Alright. We'll get started right away," she replies, flipping through my chart. "What would you like to be tested for?"

Reign did not specify what STIs she wanted me to get tested for.

"Mr. James?" the nurse repeats, looking up from the chart.

"Just test me for everything."

A look of concern flashes across her face. "Are you worried about something specific?"

I shake my head, playing it cool by using my acting chops. "No, just being cautious. I'm dating a beautiful woman, and we both agreed to get tested before becoming sexually active."

The nurse nods, and I can tell she's trying to maintain a neutral expression. She takes my vitals and asks me a few routine questions.

"Alright, I'll include a full panel of STI tests in your order. I'll be back," she says, leaving the room.

As I wait for her to return, I receive a text from Reign.

She must live in the city because she keeps suggesting meeting there. *Fuck.* I think I only have one ride left on my metro card. I can't afford to keep meeting in the city. At least not until I get my first payment. *Manhattan is expensive.*

The nurse returns with a form, handing it to me. "Please complete this form before I prepare you for testing. I'll be back in a few minutes to check in on you."

I look over the form, and it's basic questions like: Have you ever been tested for STIs and HIV? I check yes. Have you ever been diagnosed with an STI in the past? I check no. I thumb through the rest of the questions, checking no to most of them, and hand it back to the nurse when she returns.

She quickly reviews the form. "Everything looks good," she says. "I'll go ahead and prepare you for the following: HIV, herpes, syphilis, gonorrhea, and chlamydia. Additionally, I'll swab your throat since you participate in oral sex." She glances at me before continuing. "We have rapid HIV testing available, so you'll have your results in about twenty minutes. The results for the other STIs will be available within forty-eight hours, or it can take up to two weeks. The throat swab results can take anywhere from four hours to four days. What is the best contact information for you?"

"My cellphone. I wrote down my number on the form," I reply.

"Great. Do you have any questions for me?"

I shake my head, no, and she nods before proceeding with the testing. "Just relax. It will be over before you know it."

As soon as the nurse finishes, I immediately grab my phone and send Reign a text, notifying her it's done. She responds with a thumbs-up emoji. She wants to be cautious, and it's better to be safe than sorry.

Feeling a sense of calm, I relax my shoulders and gather my things to head back home.

Chapter 6: Reign

Dion left a lasting impression on me. He is unlike any man I've ever met. His choice to put his goals ahead of pursuing a relationship is an admirable quality that sets him apart from others. I don't know what I was expecting when I met him; however, I certainly wasn't expecting to hit it off so well. It's a shame that our connection will only remain professional.

"Good morning, Nancy," I say, walking into my boutique.

"Good morning, Ms. Brown. Here is your caramel latte, just the way you like it," she says with a smile.

Taking a sip of the warm drink, I thank her for always brightening my mornings. *It's going to be a wonderful day!* I assure myself.

As I start my daily routine, reviewing my emails and checking my schedule, my thoughts shift to Dion again. He seems different from other men I have dated or spoken to. There is a genuine and delightful aura that surrounds him.

My phone beeps, taking me out of my reverie. Ms. Daniels is my Valentine's Day theme bride and my only client for today. Releasing a breath of excitement, I brim with anticipation. I won't let my previous meeting with Ms. Robertson dampen my confidence, and I can't wait to show Ms. Daniels the effort I've put into making her dream wedding a reality. She is one of my unique brides, and I have a feeling today is going to be extra special.

Thumbing through my binder, I double-check all the details to ensure everything is perfect for her visit. I really want to knock it out of the park with her. She requested an unconventional wedding dress in black, and I know what you're thinking—it is a rather odd choice. When you think of Valentine's Day, you think of red or pink—not black. But for her, she is breaking tradition. It was a challenge that I gladly accepted. She couldn't decide between a mermaid dress or a princess dress. I presented her with six options: Three mermaid and three princess dresses. When she didn't like any of those, I selected another set of options. She didn't like those either, so I called in a favor from my favorite bridal boutique, Kia-che, and she kindly agreed to send me three more dresses. Hopefully, she likes one of them. My brides usually have an idea of what they want by now; however, Ms. Daniels is a unique case, and we are cutting it close to the wedding date.

When planning a wedding, it is essential to consider the budget, venue, dress, tuxedo, shoes, centerpieces, cake, and vendors (photographer, videographer, and florist). We start the decision-making process after my brides have completed a detailed questionnaire. I like to keep my brides involved in every step of the planning process, but I do the heavy lifting, and they give the final approval on all decisions.

I pull out a black and white duffle bag from the closet. Each couple is assigned a bag filled with carefully selected items for their special day. This way, they have options to consider without feeling overwhelmed. Glancing at the clock, I realize that Ms. Daniels will arrive in twenty minutes. I double-check my checklist *again* to ensure everything is in order for her appointment. *There is no room for error!* What sets Ms. Daniels apart from my previous appointment is that she hired me as her wedding planner, while Ms. Robertson was just a prospective client. Which means there's a different protocol in place.

Skylar walks into my office, her engagement ring shining on her ring finger, and I swallow the knot forming in my throat. She has several personalities depending on who she's with. Skylar has the calm, helpful, and relaxed persona with me, and then when our mother is around, she is a childish, annoying, and spoiled little bitch. When we are around our aunt and cousins, she acts like a ghost and does not say anything. She just hovers. Still, I love her all the same.

Once she started working for me, I began to see her in a different light. Not so much a brat or spoiled, but independent—*almost.*

However, since her engagement, she hasn't been pulling all of the weight that she used to. *I'm surprised she's working today.*

Skylar and Nancy assemble three foldable black tables in the center of the room. I unzip the duffel bag, and we immediately begin arranging the contents on the tables and setting up the area.

Guest books, cake knives, toasting glasses, florist options, wedding gift favors, centerpieces, and decorations are all carefully laid out for Ms. Daniels and her fiancé to review and make the final selections for their wedding. Once we've finalized everything, I'll go to the venue and coordinate with the vendors to ensure all is set for the big day. After that, I scheduled a meeting with Dion at a lovely French restaurant to have him sign the contract for our arrangement. I also need to get to know Dion better because my friends will meet him on Friday.

"Sky, could you please get the three dresses from the bridal room?"

"Sure thing," she replies, promptly heading to the bridal room to retrieve the dresses.

The sound of the buzzer at the door announces the arrival of Ms. Daniels and her fiancé.

"Nancy, would you please go greet them at the door and show them to the waiting room while I finish up with Sky?"

Nancy nods and proceeds to the front door to greet them.

Skylar returns with the dresses just as Nancy leaves to greet our clients. We hang the dresses on the rack and prepare for Ms. Daniels to join us. The first dress is a strapless mermaid style, primarily white, with a black bow around the waist and black roses wrapping around the dress from top to bottom. Despite the dress being predominantly white, the black rose wrapped around it creates the illusion of a nearly black dress. The second dress is a black mermaid lace with a sweetheart neckline and an adjustable train. The third dress is a black strapless with silver sequins running from top to bottom and a high split on the side.

Skylar escorts Ms. Daniels into my office, and she places her hands on her face and gasps in awe at the stunning dresses. "Wow, Reign! You've outdone yourself. I cannot believe how beautiful these dresses are!"

"Thank you so much, Ms. Daniels. I'm glad you like them."

Kissing her from cheek to cheek. "Let's get you into these dresses and see how they look on you!"

Ms. Daniels agrees and begins examining each dress closely. "I didn't think I would like a white wedding dress, but this one with the black bow is absolutely gorgeous. Who is the designer?"

With a proud smile, I say, "Kia is an up-and-coming designer. I fell in love with her work, and I knew you would, too." It appears that she has already made her decision, as I notice her eyes sparkling at the third dress. "Which one would you like to try first? Or should we start with the third one with the split?" I suggest, pointing to the strapless black dress on the rack that caught her eye.

Ms. Daniels nods enthusiastically and reaches for the black dress with a smile. "I love the split!"

"Great choice!" I reply, assembling the foldable gold privacy screen for her to change behind. "You're going to look stunning in that," I say, handing her the dress.

She steps behind the privacy screen and emerges a few minutes later, twirling in front of the mirror with a grin. "Oh my gosh, Reign! I love this dress!"

"I'm so glad you love it!" I say, watching as she admires herself in the mirror. "I will schedule a fitting for you at Kia's boutique. I also selected pairs of shoes that I thought would go perfectly for whichever dress you decided on. You can try them on at the fitting."

Ms. Daniels beams with excitement, thanking me profusely for my help. "You're incredible, Reign! You truly made this experience less stressful for me." She hugs me tight, tears welling up in her eyes.

This is why I love what I do—creating memorable

moments for my clients brings me so much joy.

"Thank you, Ms. Daniels. I'm just happy to help make your day even more special," I say with a smile. "But we're not done yet! Change back into your clothes, and I'll have my assistant take the dress back to Kia's boutique. We still have to decide on cake knives and other small details for your big day."

Ms. Daniels nods, her smile reaching her eyes. When she is done changing, her soon-to-be husband joins us in the room to discuss the last details together. Once everything is finalized, I head to the venue to deliver their wedding preparations and ensure everything is on track. After meeting with the coordinator at the venue, I quickly stop by my office to check my checklist and ensure I haven't overlooked anything. There are still a few crucial tasks left before the wedding, like selecting a cardboard box for cards. Before heading out to meet Dion, I make a note on my calendar to collect one during my next errand run.

Dion pulls up to the restaurant in a taxi dressed in gray slacks and a white button-up shirt with a single black rose. He smiles when our eyes meet, revealing a dimple on his left cheek. My heart swoons as he approaches, handing me the black rose, and I take a whiff of its sweet scent.

"Thank you," I say, feeling a rush of warmth in my cheeks.

"Only the best for my girl," he replies with a smile tugging at the corners of his lips.

He has really nice lips.

Choking back the butterflies in my stomach, I compliment, "Very smooth."

His smile widens, and he offers me his arm as we walk into the restaurant together.

We are seated at an intimate table by the window, and the hostess hands us the menus.

As I browse the menu, I notice Dion stealing glances at me. Clearing my throat, I look up and catch his eye. "Do I have something on my face?"

He chuckles and shakes his head. "Have you been here before?"

"Yes, plenty of times."

"I see." His jaw tightens slightly.

Wondering what he's thinking, I tilt my head to the side. "What is it?"

He scratches the back of his neck, hesitating before speaking. "I don't spend much time in the city, so I'm not familiar with many places."

"Is Manhattan not your scene?" I ask, genuinely curious. He's an actor, after all, so I assumed he visited frequently.

Dion lets out a nervous chuckle and admits, "Not really. It's too expensive for me to come here often." He takes a sip of his water to hide his discomfort.

"I guess you can say that," I reply with a modest shrug, realizing that Dion isn't as familiar with Manhattan as I had assumed. "And it helps that my father is one of the best pediatric surgeons."

He chokes on his water.

"Are you okay?"

"Yeah, I'm fine," he replies, clearing his throat. "That's impressive. It's nice to see a Black, um, well-off family."

"Thank you. My father worked hard to get where he is. Usually, Black families have to be in the entertainment industry or sports to reach that sort of success."

When our eyes meet, I feel a rush of embarrassment as I internally cringe at my poor choice of words. "I mean no disrespect by that, with the whole acting thing and whatnot."

He waves off my apology. "None taken."

Feeling mortified, I change the subject to business. I take the contract out of my bag and slide it across the table. "Let's go over the terms of our arrangement."

He nods and shifts his focus to the document in front of him.

We go over the details of the contract, discussing the payment timeline, his attendance at events with me, when we will *break* up, and the rules for kissing.

Handing Dion a pen, I point to the signature line. "If everything looks good to you, go ahead and sign on the dotted line."

After a quick scan of the document, Dion signs his name. "What are you ordering?"

He hands the contract back to me with a smile, and I put it away in my bag.

Smiling back at him. "Do you like seafood?

His eyes light up, and he nods. "I love seafood."

"Me too," I reply with a grin. "We can share the Maine Lobster Verrine. It's my favorite."

His smile widens. "Sounds delicious."

I signal the waiter to come over and take our order. "We'll have the Maine Lobster Verrine to start, please."

He nods and heads back to the kitchen.

"Dinner is on me tonight," I tell him.

He chuckles, and I screw up my face. "What's so funny?"

"It's nothing. I'll have to return the favor next time."

"Deal," I say, taking out a mini lavender notepad from my bag.

Dion raises an eyebrow.

"Tell me more about yourself." He laughs again, and I roll my eyes. "Seriously, what's the joke?"

Dion shakes his head, still smiling. "Nothing, I swear. What would you like to know, Reign?"

Nodding my head, I cast a wary look his way and then hand him a black notepad. We meet each other's gaze before laughing a little. "Okay, I see how this looks. I just thought we could ask questions and write down each other's answers."

He chuckles, flipping to a blank page. "Good idea. Can I borrow your pen again?"

Looking through my bag, I grab an extra pen and hand it across the table to him. "When is your birthday?"

"August 8th, 1990," he answers, and I jot it down.

"When is yours?"

"My birthday just passed. It was on May 8th. And I was born a year after you." I reply, watching him write down my birthday.

"So, we were both born on the eighth. That's very interesting."

"What makes it so interesting? It's just a coincidence."

He shrugs his shoulders. "I don't know. Maybe there is something there; maybe it's nothing. Perhaps we have some cosmic connection or..." He trails off. "Ah, who knows? I just think it's pretty cool."

Rolling my eyes, I move on to the next question. "What's your favorite color?"

A sexy smile spreads across his face, and his dimple appears. "Sunset."

Confusion flickers across my face. "Sunset? What dude says their favorite color is sunset?"

He chuckles, pointing to himself. "This dude right here. What's your favorite color?"

I start laughing, and Dion folds his arms across his chest. "What's the joke?"

"Nothing, nothing," I say between giggles. "My favorite color is all shades of purple."

His lips curl into a smirk. "*All* shades, huh? I haven't noticed."

"Yeah, yeah," I reply, rolling my eyes playfully.

The waiter appears with our appetizer, interrupting our banter.

"Enjoy," he says with a smile before walking away.

Dion places the napkin on his chest instead of his lap, and a small smile tugs at the corner of my mouth as I reach for a bite of the appetizer.

We continue our conversation and laughter while enjoying our food.

Chapter 7: Dion

Reign orders us the Green-Walk Hatchery Trout, grilled with baby bok choy, young radishes, rhubarb, and saga sake-pepper emulsion. I've never had it before, but Reign assures me it's good. As she orders our entrées, I find it hard to focus on what she is saying because I am distracted by watching her lips move. *This is wrong.* She is paying me for my services—a job that I intend to do well. This is an acting role and nothing more, yet I find myself wanting to rub my thumb over her plump lips just to see if they are as soft as they look.

"We should go over the events that I need you to attend with me," she says, snapping me out of my inappropriate thoughts.

Dion, pull yourself together! I discreetly shift in my seat, suppressing my arousal triggered by the sound of her voice.

"Sure," I reply, clearing my throat to regain my composure.

She gives me a weird look; however, she doesn't press on any further. "There will be a meet-and-greet with my friends on Friday, and eventually, you will meet my family before the wedding."

She screws up her face as if she's unsure about the idea of introducing me to her family.

Noticing her sudden change in expression, I ask, "Are you okay?"

Reign pauses, nervously biting her lips. "My mom and cousins are bitches. My sister is also a bit of a wild card. I'm just anxious about how they'll react to you. Or how you'll react to them."

"I'll be on my best behavior," I reassure her with a smile. "I can handle a few..." I hesitate, clearing my throat.

"Bitches." She fills in.

From a young age, my mother instilled in me the importance of never calling a woman out of their name, so I don't.

Nodding my head toward Reign. "Yeah."

That gets a chuckle out of her, and she relaxes slightly. "Good to know," she says. "We have my sister's engagement party, the wedding rehearsal dinner, her birthday, and the wedding." She briefly gazes up at the ceiling before refocusing on her notepad. "I don't know if she'll have her birthday and rehearsal dinner the same week. Or the same day. Actually, I don't know much about her wedding. I'm not even a bridesmaid, and she's my sister," she scoffs. "Anyways, after their honeymoon, you can return to your life before meeting me." Reign says the last sentence quietly, almost as an afterthought.

As she wraps up informing me of the upcoming events, she glances up at me, her lips curling into a subtle smile. Her smile is beautiful, and it warms my heart. Suddenly, a pang of sadness hits me as I'm reminded once more that this is just a professional relationship and nothing more.

Shaking the thought away, I nod to mask my disappointment and make a note of the events. "Sounds like we have a busy few months ahead."

"Yeah, it definitely will be," she replies, closing her notepad.

The waiter returns with our meals, setting them down in front of us, and we dig in.

The trout has a subtle flavor and is less fishy than some of the other seafood dishes I've tried. I let the flavors dance on my palate, and a slight smile tugs at the corners of my lips.

"The trout is good, isn't it?" She beams.

I savor another bite before replying, "Absolutely delicious."

After devouring her meal, Reign eagerly reaches for her notepad, ready to continue her probing. "I have a few more questions for you."

"Fire away," I say, finishing my last bite of trout.

"What is your favorite food other than seafood?"

Before answering, I take a refreshing sip of water to cleanse my palate. "Definitely mac and cheese," I reply. I grab my notepad as well. "What about you?"

"I actually don't have a favorite food," she admits.

"You don't?" I chuckle, finding it hard to believe.

"See, Dion James, I am going to get very annoyed with you soon if you keep laughing at me."

Realizing she's serious, I cover my mouth to hide my amusement. "My apologies. It's just that everyone has a favorite food."

She crosses her arms. "Well, I'm not like everyone else."

"Yeah, I can see that." I grin, enjoying the way her face screws up when she's annoyed.

She continues her questions by asking, "What's your favorite vegetable?"

"Spinach."

Reign peeks up at me with a raised eyebrow. "Interesting choice," she comments. "But, before you ask the same question, I'd like to finish my list."

"Go ahead."

"What is your favorite activity? Sport? And animal?"

"My favorite activity and sport is basketball." Her eyes widen at my response. It's not all that surprising, considering my height and build. "And my favorite animal is an elephant."

She burst into laughter. "An elephant, really?"

Leaning forward, I bring my hands together and a smile plays on my lips. "Yes, really. Did you know African savanna elephants are the largest species of elephant? They are easily—"

"Dude, are you seriously about to school me in the history of elephants?" She cuts me off, still snickering.

"I mean, they're pretty fascinating creatures."

She shakes her head, still giggling, and says, "I'll take your word for it. However, you can't have an elephant as a pet."

"True. But you didn't ask about my favorite pet; you asked about my favorite animal," I say with a grin.

Her smile drops, and she leans forward. My eyes involuntarily fall on her perky breast as her nipple peeks through the lace material of her top. *Damn, what I wouldn't give to...* I trail off, realizing my thoughts have strayed to a forbidden place once again.

"Okay, smart ass. What is your favorite *pet*?" She asks, bringing my attention back to the conversation.

Stroking my chin hairs, I reply, "A cat. Your turn."

"My favorite vegetable is asparagus, my favorite animal and pet are dogs, and I also enjoy playing basketball."

Impressed that she plays ball, I smile at her unexpected response. "I never would have guessed that you play ball. That's quite sexy, Reign Brown."

She blushes at my unexpected compliment, taking a sip of her drink to hide her flustered reaction. "Well, thank you, Dion James. Maybe one day you'll see me in action on the court."

Reign is my dream girl—beautiful, intelligent, funny, and athletic. *Damn!* I have to keep reminding myself that this isn't real and that it's just business between us.

As the evening progressed, we exchanged stories and got to know each other better. Eventually, she scribbled her home address on a piece of paper and passed it to me. And just as I suspected, she lives in the area.

Reign Brown is way out of my league.

Friday
May 17th, 2024

Chapter 8: Dion

My room is a chaotic mess, with clothes scattered everywhere as if a tornado passed through it. I'm trying to figure out what to wear tonight to impress Reign's friends. She told me to dress casually, but I'm not sure if her casual and my casual are the same. The two times we met in person, she wore professional clothing that clung to her curves in the right places. All of the blood rushes to my cock, thinking of her sexy body. I've never had such an instant attraction to a woman. It feels unnatural. Still, everything about Reign turns me on. She's different from anyone I've ever met. *What is wrong with me?* I bite my knuckles to get a grip on reality. This. Is. Pretend.

How can I expect anyone in the acting world to take me seriously if I can't even pretend to be someone's boyfriend? Acting requires talent and commitment to a storyline, and Reign is just a character.

She is paying me to do a job, and I need to focus on delivering a convincing performance. *My attraction is part of the act and not real.* I repeat to myself.

Opting for black slacks and a tan button-up shirt, I pick up the single black rose from the counter and head out. The first time I saw her in the bar, she had a gold bracelet on her left wrist with a single black rose on it. She wore the same bracelet when we met in Central Park.

When I arrive at Reign's home, I'm granted access by the doorman. I expected nothing less from a woman of her status. As I make my way inside, I remind myself to stay in character and not let my attraction to her interfere with the job. Gathering my thoughts, I summon the courage to knock on her door, taking in a sharp breath and then letting it out. As she opens the door, my eyes are immediately drawn to her figure, slowly taking in every curve and contour. Her braids are pulled into a high bun, and her skin glistens as if she had just stepped out of the shower. She's dressed in black shorts and a white V-neck t-shirt, and her perky nipples are visible through the thin fabric. I try to maintain eye contact while handing her the rose. If I can't handle pretending to be her man, how can I possibly handle being in the same room with an actress? I don't get it. I've had the opportunity to kiss other women in commercials, beautiful and sexy women, but none of them have made me feel this way.

She smiles, thanking me for the rose and inviting me inside. "Are you going to give me a rose every time you see me?"

Looking around Reign's apartment, purple was definitely

her favorite color.

A smirk forms on my lips. "Maybe. Do you not like roses?"

Her smile widens. "No, I love roses. I actually wear a bracelet with a rose on it." She pauses, a thought seemingly crossing her mind before she continues, "Wait, have you noticed my bracelet before? Is that why you're giving me roses?"

Realizing she caught on to my subtle gesture, I snort. "And here I thought I was being romantic."

She brings the velvety rose to her nose, inhaling its sweet fragrance, and smiles softly. "No, you definitely are. Let me show you around."

I follow her lead into the living room, taking in the cozy ambiance of her place. She points to the balcony. "We are going to have drinks out there when my friends arrive."

"You have a beautiful home," I remark.

"Thank you. It wasn't easy."

"I didn't imagine it would be."

"I used my trust fund to furnish the place; however, I worked my ass off to pay for the down payment myself, not to mention that I paid for my first apartment on my own as well," she explains before stopping herself. "Sorry, sometimes I tend to ramble."

"Don't apologize. It's impressive that you've accomplished so much on your own," I comment, genuinely impressed.

"I'm aware that not many people have the same opportunities as me. Still, I didn't want to grow up being a spoiled little brat like my sister." Reign looks off into the distance, a shadow passing over her face before quickly changing the subject. "Anyway, let me give you the rundown of my friends." She leads me into the kitchen, where she has more little notepads sitting on the countertop. She leaps onto the island and sits while I rest my elbows on the ledge, trying my best not to stare too much at her breast.

"Your friend Eddie and my friend Scarlette are the only ones who know about our little arrangement." She looks at me to confirm, and I nod. "When Scarlette comes tonight, she'll pretend she's never met you. My only other friend, August, who has been happily married since college, is also coming. And so are my sister Skylar and her friend Darcy." She rolls her eyes, clearly not thrilled about Darcy tagging along. "Between you and me, I don't really like Darcy. I don't know why, but my spirit doesn't take to her."

My lips curl into a grin, taking in all of the information about her friends.

"Oh snap!" Reign exclaims, looking at the clock on the microwave above the stove. "They'll be here in about thirty minutes. I'm sorry for talking your ear off."

"No worries. This is stuff a boyfriend should know about his girlfriend, right?"

Her gaze meets mine, and it's like time stands still. "Yeah," she slowly replies before jumping off the island. "I have to get dressed."

Isn't she dressed already?

My thoughts must be on my face because she looks me over from head to toe and folds her arms across her chest.

"Stay here. I am not wearing this when you're dressed like that. I'll be back in a minute."

She disappears into the bedroom, leaving me standing in the living room. I look at all of the photos on the walls of her and, I assume, her family. She seems happy in the pictures with a man, I think is her father, but not so much in the pictures with two women. I'm guessing they are her sister and mother. Or maybe these are the cousins she was telling me about. There are photos of her wearing a basketball uniform and holding medals and trophies. She wasn't kidding when she said she plays basketball.

"Hey, can you zip me up?"

I whip around to see her standing there in a fitted beige dress that perfectly accentuates her curves.

"Sure," I reply, standing behind her and inhaling her intoxicating scent. I carefully zip up her dress, trying to keep my cool despite the warmth of her body against mine and the way the fabric hugs her figure. Reign has no idea what she is doing to me. I clear my throat and take a step back, only to discover that my dick is straining against my pants.

She turns around to thank me.

"Where is your bathroom?"

"Down the hall to the right," she replies, clearly unaware of the effect she has on me.

I quickly excuse myself and hurry to the bathroom, closing the door behind me. The sweet scent of vanilla wafts through the air. I look down at my throbbing erection, which shows no sign of subsiding. *I feel like a creep.* Taking a piece of toilet paper, I unzip my pants and firmly grasp the shaft. I begin the motion by slowly gliding my hand up and down. As I close my eyes and imagine the way her dress clung to her ass, I quicken my pace. I wonder what it would feel like to be inside her and to hear her moan my name. The thought alone pushes me closer to the edge, my breaths coming in short gasps. With a final stroke, I release. *Fuck!* I am extremely attracted to her.

Staring at my reflection in the mirror, I wash my hands, clean myself up, and splash cold water on my face. I need to focus and keep my physical attraction to her in check, no matter how sexy she is.

Think with your head, not with your cock.

Drying my face, I head back to the living room, where Reign's waiting for me.

While walking back, I admire the awards and achievements proudly showcased on the walls. Even if my intentions were not to pursue an acting career and maintain this facade for her benefit, I doubt my ability to measure up to a man worthy of someone as exceptional as her.

When I return to the living room, I'm greeted by her friends.

"So, this is the infamous Dion!" One of the women exclaims, circling me with a curious smile.

Sporting a charismatic grin, I skillfully keep up the pretense of being the ideal gentleman in front of her friend. "Yes, that's me. And who might you be?"

"I'm August," she replies, extending her hand for a shake. Ah, she's the married one.

"It's nice to meet you, August," I respond, shaking her hand.

"Likewise," she replies, her smile widening.

"And I'm Escarletta Lucia Rodriguez," Scarlette introduces herself, smiling from ear to ear. "But you can call me Scarlette."

Suppressing a laugh, I let out a slight cough.

Reign rolls her eyes at Scarlette's dramatic introduction. "She is so extra."

With a slight smirk, I nod politely and Scarlette gives me a knowing look.

"Nice to meet you, Scarlette." I say, keeping up the charade of not recognizing each other.

Reign and I exchange glances before she introduces her sister Skylar and her friend Darcy.

"Ladies, it's nice to meet you both."

Skylar nods before brushing past me and onto the balcony while Darcy looks me over from head to toe, a crease forming between her brows. "I find it odd that Reign hasn't mentioned you before." She looks between Reign and me, her eyes narrowing slightly. "Until Skylar announced she was getting married."

Darcy's words hang in the air, causing a shift in the atmosphere. Reign has a panicked look in her eyes as she tries to come up with a response. I quickly wrap my arm around her waist and pull her closer to me before she can speak.

"Well, now you know." Reign visibly relaxes against me, and to take it up a notch, I lean in to press my lips against hers, causing both Reign and Darcy to gasp in surprise and Scarlette and August's mouths to drop open.

Reign's lips soften under mine, and her hand grips the fabric of my shirt as she kisses me back. I slide my tongue along her bottom lip, deepening the kiss, feeling her heartbeat quicken against my chest. Kissing her exceeds all of my expectations, and I feel a rush of emotions that I never knew were possible. However, what I really want is for this kiss to be genuine, not just a show for Darcy. I pull back slightly, and there's a blush spreading across Reign's cheeks as she looks at me with wide eyes.

Turning my attention to Darcy. "Sorry for not telling you sooner."

Darcy rolls her eyes and mutters something under her breath before joining Skylar on the balcony.

Reign is staring at me in stunned silence while I overhear August whispering to Scarlette, "I like him," as they head to the kitchen to grab a drink.

Before I can start apologizing to her when we are alone, Reign surprises me by pulling me into a tight hug. Her smile reaches her eyes when she says, 'Thank you for doing that for me."

Wrapping my arms around her. "That's what fake boyfriends are for, right?"

She chuckles softly into my chest before pulling away and looking me in the eyes. "You're doing a pretty good job at it."

Reign doesn't realize how easy it is to pretend to be in a relationship with someone as amazing as her. It almost feels natural, like we could actually be a real couple. I smile back at her, and she leads us to the balcony to join the others.

Chapter 9: Reign

Watching Dion blend in with my friends ignites my imagination, painting vivid pictures of the incredible bond we could share if our relationship took a romantic turn. And the way he handled Darcy's comment to defend me was so epic. My lips still tingle from our kiss. It was so unexpected, yet it felt like time stood still, and I keep replaying it in my mind.

August talks about her constant vacation readiness while Dion smiles and nods. I subtly catch Scarlette's attention by gesturing my head toward the kitchen. We slip away from the balcony, leaving Dion behind with the rest of the group.

Scarlette's eyes light up with excitement when we are alone. "Okay, spill! What happened out there?"

"I don't even know where that came from. It just felt right in the moment," I say with a shy smile. "How do you think Dion is doing out there with everyone?"

Her grin widens as she responds, "Oh, my gosh! He is doing so well! I almost thought he was your real boyfriend for a second there."

Her teasing makes me blush, but I'm relieved that Dion is fitting in with the group.

"And the way he kissed you and made eye contact with that bitch!" She adds, making a kissing gesture with her hand. "Icing on the cake."

I agree with a nervous laugh, and we link arms to walk back to the balcony. Skylar and Darcy are lost in their conversation, ignoring Dion and August, which is fine because August is animatedly chatting about Calvin with him. Seeing the joy on her face as she talks about the love of her life gives me a glimmer of hope that there is a person out there for everyone.

I sit next to Dion, and August excuses herself to get another drink, leaving us alone. Dion slides his arm around my waist, pulling me closer and tugging at my heartstrings.

Trying to play it cool, I nudge his shoulder. "What are you doing next Friday?"

He chuckles and responds, "I'm sure you're about to tell me."

I swat his chest, and he catches my hand, intertwining our fingers. I stare at our tangled hands before meeting his gaze. "Um, I was wondering if you could come with me to my family dinner."

"Anything for my girl," he replies, a sexy smile playing on his lips and his left dimple visible.

My heart flutters at his response, and Scarlette and August exchange knowing glances across the balcony, squealing. Skylar and Darcy break away from their conversation to look over at us, and Darcy rolls her eyes.

Dion notices everyone watching us, and a seductive smile crosses his lips. He surprises me by pulling me onto his lap and wrapping his arms around my waist. Blushing at his bold move, I feel a subtle shift beneath me, but I decide to disregard it. Men can't always control their physical reactions. He is acting, and his body is responding naturally to my ass sitting on him.

Skylar and Darcy share an annoyed glance while Scarlette and August watch Dion and me with amused expressions.

"Well, this has been fun. However, it's time to go," Darcy announces, standing up and pulling Skylar along with her.

Why is my sister friends with her?

I give them a tight-lipped smile.

"I'll see you at dinner tomorrow, Reign," Skylar says, looking past me to Dion and adding, "It's a family-only event."

"I'll see you tomorrow," I respond, rolling my eyes as they walk away.

"I'm going to leave, too," August says. "It was very nice meeting you, Dion."

"Nice meeting you too, August," Dion replies with a charming smile, and I wave goodbye to her.

When she leaves, I quickly jump off his lap, creating some space between us.

Scarlette claps her hands together. "And end scene!" she laughs.

He looks amused at my sudden movement, and I shoot Scarlette a playful glare.

"You two are adorable," she comments, and my cheeks flush as Dion stands up as well, burying his hands in his pockets.

Scarlette nudges him, saying, "You are doing great, Dion."

He shrugs, a small smile playing on his lips. "Thank you, I guess."

"No, seriously! You're a natural at this," she insists. "For a quick moment, I actually thought you were my best friend's real boyfriend, and the way you kissed her was just wow, so swoon-worthy!"

His smile fades slightly at her words, and he avoids my gaze, looking a bit uncomfortable. *What is that about?*

Scarlette doesn't notice and continues to gush about his acting skills. With a gentle brush of my elbow, I silently communicate to her to stop.

When she catches on, she glances at her phone and blurts out, "Oh, look at the time! I'll catch you guys later." With a quick wave, she hurries off, leaving Dion and me standing there in an awkward silence.

To break the tension between us, I clear my throat. "So, how about we clean up this mess?"

He nods in response.

We start gathering the empty plates and cups, avoiding each other's gaze as we work in silence. While we are cleaning, I catch him stealing glances at me from the corner of my eye; however, I can't quite figure out what he's thinking.

"Thank you for tonight," I say, breaking the silence.

He looks up at me and says, "No problem, I'm just doing my job." I watch him knot the trash bag and tie it up. "It was a pleasure meeting your friends."

Quirking an eyebrow. "Was it?"

Dion chuckles. "Well, maybe not all of them," he admits with a smirk. "Scarlette and August are great, but your sister pretty much avoided me, and Darcy is rude."

Bursting into laughter, I hold my stomach. "Well, don't hold back on my account."

"I just call it like I see it," he says with a shrug. "I don't mean to be rude."

Shaking my head, I giggle. "No worries. Skylar is a little standoffish at first; however, Darcy is definitely not the friendliest person. She's only around because she's Sky's friend. I have never liked Darcy since the first day I met her, but my mother adores and treats her better than me. Darcy is like the other daughter my mom has always wanted."

Dion's expression softens as he walks over to me, taking my hand in his. "I'm sorry."

Shrugging my shoulders, I peek up at him with a weak smile. A small tear wells up in the corner of my eye, and despite my efforts to contain it, it trickles down my cheek. Dion tenderly wipes it away with his thumb. If only he knew how much my mother sucked. I stare at our joined hands. I wish I could tell him about the blatant favoritism my mother shows towards my sister without him feeling sorry for me. She has always made it clear that Skylar was her favorite, and no matter how hard I tried, I could never measure up in her eyes. We also have nothing in common. I remember when Sky was born, a switch flipped in my mother's heart as if she had only enough love for one child. As I grew up, I was a tomboy, while Skylar always wore decorated dresses and bows. My mother never attended any of my basketball games or showed any interest in what I wanted to do, and she had no excuse for not being there because she was a stay-at-home mom. Still, she was always front and center at every dance recital and fashion show my sister participated in. As busy as my father was, he made every effort to attend at least three of my games per season. But when he couldn't make it to the games, I had no family in the stands cheering me on. Scarlette and her family were there, but it would have been nice to have my parents and sister there as well.

Dion gently lifts my chin to meet his gaze. "Hey, are you okay?"

The inner turmoil in my head threatens to spill out; however, I force a smile. "No, but I will be. I'll add it to the list of things to discuss with my therapist."

There's a surprised expression on his face. "You have a therapist?"

"Yes, I started seeing one to work out some...personal issues."

"Does it...help?"

A small smile tugs at the corner of my lips. "More than you know."

Dion looks at me with an unreadable expression before nodding slowly. "I'm glad you're taking care of yourself."

We stare at each other for a moment longer, lost in a comfortable silence.

"You should probably go," I finally say, breaking the quietness between us.

I guide him towards the door, attempting a handshake that he quickly turns into an unexpected and comforting hug.

"Goodnight, Reign," he says before placing a soft kiss on my cheek that sends a shiver down my spine and an ache between my thighs.

"Goodnight, Dion," I whisper back.

Closing the door behind me and twisting the locks, I lean against the door and rub my fingers over my lips, thinking about the kiss we shared earlier.

He's a great kisser.

Walking to my bedroom, I replay the memory of his lips on mine, and a sudden urge for release washes over me. As I lie down on my bed, I slide off my black lacey underwear, casually tossing it on the floor. I reach for Rocky in my bedside drawer, then spread my legs open and slide my fingers along the slickness of my sex. Closing my eyes, I imagine the sensation of Dion's hands on my skin and how it would feel on my pussy. Reminiscing about our kiss, I firmly press Rocky against my clit, hoping for some relief; however, the batteries are dead. My eyes snap open, prompting me to open my nightstand drawer and search for new batteries. You've got to be kidding me!

I'm all out of batteries. Frustrated, I throw myself back onto my pillow.

This is some shit.

Dion's kiss lingers on my lips, intensifying the ache between my legs.

Maybe I should take a cold shower.

I step into the shower and detach the showerhead, adjusting the pressure to the highest setting to intensify the sensation on my clit, ultimately bringing me to a shuddering climax. I lean against the tile, catching my breath as the tension releases from my body. Feeling satisfied and relaxed, I step out of the shower and dry off, changing into pajamas. I'll make sure to stock up on batteries next time. Crawling into bed, I close my eyes.

The showerhead did the job, but I want the real thing inside me.

Saturday
May 18th, 2024

Chapter 10: Reign

Getting ready for family dinner is much more difficult when my kiss with Dion is still fresh in my mind. The warmth of his soft, juicy lips against mine lingers, causing me to bite my bottom lip gently. I went to bed relieved after my cold shower; however, I woke up feeling restless, replaying the moment over and over in my mind. I absentmindedly lick my lips, still feeling the gentle caress of his tongue. The kiss was so soft and sensual.

Every touch, every movement, and every breath were etched in my mind, making it difficult to focus on anything else. As I imagine his hands exploring the curves of my body, an involuntary moan escapes my lips, and the sound of my voice startles me.

Part of me wants to forget it ever happened, while another part of me wishes I could relive it over and over and *over* again.

I have three missed calls from my sister. As I glance at the time, I realize that if I don't request an Uber now, I will be late. Sucking my teeth in frustration, I quickly head to the bathroom to get ready and request an Uber. Before heading out, I check my appearance in the mirror. My makeup is simple, with a touch of mascara and lip balm. It's just dinner with my family to announce Skylar's wedding nuptials. There's no need to go all out.

I head out the door to the elevator. Once on the lower level, I give a slight nod of appreciation to the doorman before entering the Uber.

My parents reside in a grand, five-story home near Central Park on the Upper West Side, with six bedrooms and nine bathrooms. I don't understand why they need so many bathrooms for just the two of them. Nonetheless, it appears that my father's inclination to "spread out" is a common trait among the wealthy.

Whatever that means.

The ride is quick, and I arrive just in time for this dreadful dinner. I take a deep breath before walking through the front door, mentally preparing myself for the inevitable criticism from my mother that usually follows. The high ceilings and extravagant chandeliers greet me. My mother had a hand in overseeing every intricate detail of the renovations. The hardwood floors and the imported marble countertops were precisely chosen to reflect her expensive taste.

"Reign, thank you for gracing us with your appearance," my mother says distastefully, her eyes scanning me from head to toe. She kisses each of my cheeks, and I muster a smile.

"My beautiful Amara," my father's voice booms from across the room, his arms outstretched for a hug.

Amara signifies eternal beauty and was chosen by my father to pay tribute to his late mother.

"Hi, Dad," I say, hugging him and trying to redirect the

attention away from my mother's disapproving gaze.

"Our guests are waiting," she reminds us, clasping her hands together to hurry us to the dining table.

I follow my parents into the dining room. They hired private chefs for the evening, and waiters and waitresses in formal attire are waiting to serve us. There is an array of food, and tasty pastries lined up on the table for us to enjoy. I curtly nod at my aunt Shirl and ignore her disgusting husband. She is my mother's older sister and has been married for as long as I can remember. My aunt's husband is a retired doctor and introduced my parents to each other. My grandmother—may she rest in peace—insisted her daughters marry men with money. According to the stories my mother told us about my grandma, she grew up poor until she married into wealth. My grandma knew she wanted the same for her daughters.

I sit down in the chair next to my father on the other side of the table farthest from my stuck-up cousins.

"Oh, look what the cat dragged in," Robyn snickers, glancing in my direction.

Our gazes meet; however, I don't respond. Placing the napkin on my lap, I take a piece of bread from the basket and butter it.

"Reign is so pathetic sitting there with no husband on her arm," Raquel says to her older sister Shonda, loud enough for me to hear.

Shonda chuckles. "Who would even want her? She's old and washed up, just like her mother always said she would be."

Slamming my hands down on the table, I cause the silverware to clatter. "I can hear you!"

"Good!" Raquel retorts, not bothering to lower her voice.

"Maybe if you actually had a husband, you wouldn't be so bitter all the time."

"Ladies, stop acting like children," my mother interrupts, not to defend me but to demand everyone's attention. "This is a celebratory dinner for my beautiful daughter, Skylar. In just a few months, she will marry her prince charming, and my heart couldn't be fuller to have a wonderful soon-to-be son."

Right on cue, Skylar and Peter walk hand in hand into the dining room, smiling at everyone.

The room erupts in applause and congratulations as Skylar and Peter take their seats together.

"Thank you, everyone," Peter says, his green eyes flickering with happiness.

He leads Skylar to a seat at the table next to my cousin Raquel. Skylar screeches with excitement, showcasing her diamond ring as she waves her hand around for everyone to see.

Those bitches gasp in awe at the size of the rock on her finger, whispering to each other about how lucky Skylar is.

"Oh, Sky, your ring is absolutely gorgeous," Raquel squeals.

"Yes, Sky, it's stunning! You're going to blind us all with that bling," Shonda chimes in.

"Peter, you did a fantastic job picking out that ring," Robyn adds.

Skylar blushes and thanks them all, her smile widening as she looks down at the ring on her finger. When the chatter dies down just a little, she looks in my direction and catches my eye. "What do you think, Reign?"

"Why ask her?" Robyn mutters under her breath. "She's probably just jealous."

"Because she's my sister, and I value her opinion," Skylar says with a smile that reaches her eyes.

Eyeing Robyn warily, I smile at Skylar and say, "It's beautiful Sky. Peter really outdid himself." Skylar beams and my gaze shifts to Peter, who is running his fingers through his spikey, dark brown hair. "I can tell how much thought and effort you put into choosing it. It suits her perfectly."

Peter smirks with pride at my words. "The lovely Reign, I'm glad you think so."

"Oh, please, what's so lovely about her?" Shonda snidely says, crossing her arms.

My smile falters as I glance at her. "The mean girl routine is getting a bit old for someone pushing forty. Is that gray hair I see peeking through your roots?"

"Shut up, Reign!" Shonda retorts, her face flushing with anger.

"You first, bitch!" I quip back.

"Enough!" My mother intervenes, pushing her chair back from the table. "Why do you have to act like this, Reign? Tonight is not about you. It's about Skylar and Peter and their engagement." Glancing at Peter apologetically, she continues, "Peter, I apologize for Reign's immature behavior. She can be a handful sometimes, but we're all here to celebrate your happiness. The floor is yours."

"Sweetheart, take the high road," my father whispers to me.

My cheeks burn with embarrassment, and I exhale deeply, picking at my bread.

Peter takes Skylar's hand in his, a smile spreading across his face. "Thank you, Mrs. Brown."

Skylar squeezes Peter's hand. "We have decided to get

married the day after my birthday!" She grins from ear to ear as Peter releases her hand to wrap his arm around her waist, pulling her close.

"We chose October 25th as the perfect date because I will be turning twenty-five this year, and because of my love for Halloween, we decided to have a Halloween-themed wedding."

Peter glances at me and winks. "And we would love for Reign to plan our wedding. Just let me know the cost and—"

"Oh, nonsense, Peter! You are family," my mother interrupts. "Reign will plan your wedding for you at no cost."

I choke on my bread. *This fucking bitch.* I hit my chest to stop coughing, trying to process what my mother just said.

My father waves a server over to bring me some water while my mother looks at me disapprovingly from across the table.

Trying to compose myself, I take a few sips of my water, before responding to Peter's request. "You would like me to plan your wedding?"

That's probably why Skylar didn't mention to me who she would be selecting as maid of honor.

He looks between me and my mother. "Yes."

"Reign would be happy to help," my mother responds, silently warning me not to object.

"I am a grown woman. I can answer for myself, Mother," I say firmly, meeting her gaze head-on. "I would love to help plan their wedding; however, you can't expect to use all my resources for free."

"This is not up for discussion. You will happily plan your sister's wedding free of charge," she says.

I count to ten in my head before responding.

Arguing with my mother is pointless.

"It will be my pleasure," I say through gritted teeth, then I excuse myself from the table. "I have somewhere I need to be."

"Wait before you go," Skylar calls out. "Please make a note of the dates."

I want to roll my eyes at her request, but with everyone at the table watching, I force a smile and grab a pen and notepad from my bag to jot down the important dates. "What are the dates?"

"I would like the rehearsal dinner and my birthday dinner to be held on my birthday, Thursday, October 24th. And I want the wedding reception to be on Friday, October 25th, at 7 p.m."

I scribble down the dates and times before swiftly making my exit. As a waitress prepares a to-go box for me, my father stops me before I can leave.

"Amara, dear, can I speak with you for a moment?"

Suppressing a sigh, I clench my fists in frustration. "What is it?"

"How much money do you think you'll need to plan Sky's wedding?"

"You heard your wife. She said I was doing it for free."

He looks over his shoulder and lowers his voice. "Reign, I will write you a check. Just let me know the cost." My father only addresses me by my first name when he is serious.

"I'll get back to you on that, Dad," I concede.

"Okay, let's keep this between us."

A faint grin appears on my face. "Sure."

He kisses my forehead and walks me to the door, hugging me tight before I leave.

Wednesday
May 22ⁿᵈ, 2024

Chapter 11: Dion

From the comfort of my bed, I find myself engrossed by the patterns on the ceiling, lost in thought as I unravel the complexities of my life.

Where did I go wrong? I'm in my thirties, and I don't have my life figured out.

No wife, no kids, no actual job.

Despite my passion for acting, I have not achieved the level of success I had anticipated. I often ask myself if I have chosen the right path intended by God or if my desire is simply not meant to be fulfilled. My mind drifts to Reign. She seems to have it all together. Reign has established both a comfortable living space and a flourishing business of her own. The thought of her alone makes my dick twitch under my boxers. *Not again.*

It is common knowledge that every man wakes up with morning wood. But this...this is different. I want to bury myself deep inside Reign's pussy, feeling her walls clench against my shaft as I fuck her into next week.

The piercing sound of my alarm interrupts my inappropriate thoughts. It's already 11 a.m., and panic settles in as I realize I only have an hour before I'm supposed to meet my parents for lunch. My mom called me last night and told me that my dad would be joining us for lunch today and that they wanted to talk to me about something. *This can't be good.* I jump out of bed and head to the bathroom for a cold shower.

After my quick shower, I hastily throw on some clothes, my mind still fixated on Reign. It's frustrating how much she consumes my thoughts, especially because our relationship is meant to be professional. Instead of daydreaming about her, I need to stay committed to the act of being her boyfriend. Despite my best efforts, I'm physically attracted to her. The more I get to know her, the more I find myself drawn to her personality and intelligence as well. Shaking my head, I request an Uber. I need to pull myself together to make sure I don't keep my parents waiting.

On my way to the restaurant, I begin thinking about Reign again. *Why can't I get her out of my head?* Is she attracted to me, too, or is she just playing along for the sake of our agreement? Pushing these thoughts away for the millionth time, I check my bank account, and a grin forms on my face as I see that my first payment from Reign has cleared, reminding me that this is a business transaction. This time, I will be able to pay for lunch.

The restaurant is busier today, so our usual booth is taken. I look around for my parents, and I spot my mom seated at the back of the restaurant, waving me over.

My mom's eyes light up as I approach. "Atom!" she exclaims, kissing me on the cheek.

"Hi, Mom, how are you?" I ask, sitting down across from

her and greeting my dad with a smile.

She places her napkin on her lap and replies, "I'm doing well, dear. We missed you in church last Sunday."

Feeling a pang of guilt, I scratch the back of my neck. "Uh yeah, sorry about that…maybe I can make it this Sunday."

My mother rolls her shoulders back and eyes me warily.

"You missed a good service. The choir sounded good, and the sermon was truly inspiring," my dad adds, taking a sip of his water.

Clearing my throat. "I'm sorry I missed the service. I-I was a little busy." I stammer, scratching the back of my neck.

My mother's eyes are vast, and she shakes her head in disgust.

"Is something wrong?" I ask.

She takes a sip of her water and sets the glass down gently, her expression turning serious. "I don't know," she says slowly, folding her arms across her chest. "You tell me."

"Now, now, dear, if Dion has something to tell us, he will do it in his own time," my father says.

When my mother suspects something, she uses subtle tactics like leaning in closer or raising an eyebrow to get me to open up. However, this time, I have no idea what they are referring to.

"Mom, just tell me what's on your mind."

Her eyes narrow slightly as she studies me, and then she finally speaks. "Sister Moore told us that her daughter saw you at Central Park with some woman. Is there something you need to tell us?"

A lump forms in my throat as I try to come up with a response. I have an open and honest relationship with both of my parents. Still, I cannot tell them about Reign and my fake relationship. She would be against it, and my father wouldn't understand.

"Well…" she pauses, giving me a pointed look.

Quickly reaching for my glass of water, I take a long sip to buy myself a few extra seconds to gather my thoughts.

"Atom?"

Clearing my throat, I inhale and exhale a sharp breath. "I was at Central Park with a young woman."

Her eyes bore into me, silently urging me to continue.

I shift uncomfortably in my seat. "That's all I can say for now."

Dad's lips curl into a huge grin. "If you are happy, son, then so are we."

Mom looks pleased with my response, nodding in approval. "I hope to be a grandmother one day," she says with a wistful smile.

Dad grins from ear to ear. "It is about time."

Mom nudges Dad with her elbow and chuckles. "Shall we order?"

Looking between the two of them, I feel guilty about keeping this secret from them. Shaking my head, I force a smile. "I will have my usual."

My father signals for the waitress to come over while I send Reign a text.

With my focus now back on my parents, I put my phone in my pocket.

"We were losing hope that you would never settle down," she says.

"Well, no, you were losing hope," Dad says.

"What? No, you just said the other night that Dion was—"

"Mom, it's nothing. We're just friends. It's not that

serious," I say, cutting her off and trying my best to downplay the situation.

"Dion Atom James, you were never a good liar," she says with a knowing smile. "But I'll drop it for now. You will tell me the truth when you are ready."

The waitress arrives at our table with impeccable timing, just as my mother's interrogation seems to be coming to an end.

Eddie and Scarlette are the only people who know the truth about Reign and me. My mother is a devoted Christian; she does not believe in the art of acting and would be against our arrangement. Don't get me wrong; she enjoys watching reality housewives and soap operas, but she has reservations about her own son working in the industry. My mother believes God has a plan for everyone; however, she doesn't think that acting is for me.

As we dig into our meals, my parents inform me they are leaving for a three-week trip next week, so we will not be having lunch. Which is a relief for me, as it will give me some time to figure out what I am going to do.

The Uber driver drops me off down the block from Reign's boutique. I need the walk to gather my thoughts before meeting with her. I'm torn between whether my attraction for her is only physical or if there is a more profound connection forming between us. However, I'm not sure if I'm ready to face these emotions. Reign is paying me to be her boyfriend.

The proof is in my bank account. Still, the way my mom's face lit up, I don't want to deceive her. She seemed genuinely happy for me—they both did. And I believe the truth would devastate her. I would love to be in a real relationship, get married and have a family someday. Unfortunately, I am not financially stable enough for any of that right now.

I just need my acting career to take off.

The woman at the desk greets me as I step into Reign's boutique.

"Hello, Mr. James. Reign is expecting you. Please follow me to her office."

I fall in step behind the woman down the hallway, passing by Skylar's office as she is on the phone.

"Mom, you're not listening to what I want. And I don't want to do this!" she whisper-shouts into the phone. When she sees me, her expression changes, and she closes the door.

Shrugging it off, I enter Reign's office. She looks up from her desk, her smile fading when she notices the severe look on my face.

"Shut the door behind you," she instructs, closing the orange and black binder that is in front of her, labeled *Skylar's wedding*.

A pang of guilt settles in my chest as I awkwardly take a seat across from her.

"What do you want to talk about?"

Her eyes lock onto mine with anticipation, causing my mouth to go dry like sandpaper.

"Dion?"

Clearing my throat. "Uh, one of the sisters at my family's church. Her daughter saw us at Central Park."

A slight smirk plays on Reign's lips, and she reopens her

binder, flipping through the pages. "This is why you wanted to meet in person?" she asks, her eyes scanning the contents.

"Yes."

Reign looks up from the binder, her expression unreadable. "Dion, we are in a 'relationship.'" She says, using air quotes for the word relationship. "People are bound to see us together."

"Yes, but this 'relationship' is for your family, not mine," I remind her, gesturing air quotes as well and trying to keep my tone even. Our eyes meet, and a tense energy crackles between us. "I'm very close with my parents, especially my mother, and they should know about our arrangement. It's important to me that they understand the situation."

Reign looks away, her jaw tense, and proceeds to check off whatever is in the binder.

"Reign?"

She slams the binder shut, and her brows snap together. "No one needs to know about this. It's strictly business between us, remember? I am paying you to be my boyfriend. No one can know that. The only reason Scarlette and Eddie know is because they helped set up this arrangement. Let's keep it that way."

Ouch.

"You expect me to lie to my own parents?"

Her eyes, a beautiful shade of brown, flash with frustration, emitting a palpable intensity. The subtle sound of her exasperated sigh fills the air. "I expect you to keep our agreement confidential. How old are you? Aren't you a grown-ass man? Why do you need to tell Mommy the truth?" She retorts, her tone mocking.

Standing to my full height, I meet her gaze with a firm

expression. "It saddens me that your family requires you to lie for their acceptance. That is not how I was raised."

She stands up, her posture tense, as she looks me in the eye. "Will you keep your voice down? I don't need your judgment, just your cooperation. You knew what you were getting into when you signed the contract. You agreed to be my boyfriend until October, and you're getting paid well for this, so I suggest you keep your end of the deal. Perhaps tell your parents that you landed an acting gig and you were meeting with your co-star."

We stare at each other in a heated silence. When I signed up for this fake relationship, I never considered my parents finding out or that someone from the church would see us. When did Sister Moore's daughter start visiting the city anyway? We are from Long Island, and before deciding to pursue a career in acting, I had barely visited the town. *It's way too expensive.* However, just because I am not a city person doesn't mean Sister Moore's daughter isn't. There are plenty of things to do and see in the city that she might enjoy.

"Dion?"

I'm torn between the money and my conscience. I don't feel comfortable lying to my mother.

Perhaps I didn't thoroughly think this through before agreeing to it.

"Dion, I will offer you an additional one thousand to keep this between us," she pleads, her expression softening.

"No, it's fine. I'll figure something out," I respond, turning to leave her office.

As I reach for the door handle, she calls out, "Dion…wait."

I pause. "What is it?"

She sighs heavily and says, "I apologize for my snappy

tone.”

Turning around to meet her gaze with sincerity, I sigh as well. “I also apologize for raising my voice.”

We both stand there for a moment, silently acknowledging each other’s apologies.

“You can say you were meeting with a colleague. In a way, that’s not entirely untrue because we are working together,” she suggests with a small smile.

My lips curve upwards, mirroring the soft smile on her face. “That works.”

“I want you to meet my family this Friday for dinner. Are you still up for it?”

Nodding my head slowly. “Of course, I will meet you at your place.”

“Thank you,” she murmurs softly as I head out the door.

Chapter 12: Reign

My heart pounds in my chest in a rapid rhythm of anticipation as I imagine my parents' reactions when they meet Dion for the first time. My parents will not only consider him a boyfriend but also a potential future son-in-law. I'm a hypocrite for only worrying about what my parents will think when his parents are probably thinking the same thing about me. Suddenly, the daunting thought of us breaking up crosses my mind.

How will I break the news to them? Will they be disappointed? What will they think of me?

My mother blamed me for breaking up with Max, and she even apologized to him for my behavior. She told my sister that he cheated on me because I wasn't giving him what he needed. Her voice still echoes in my head. *"If Reign had done what she was supposed to do in her relationship, he might not have cheated."*

Why would she say that? What type of mother would say such a thing?

When the time comes for Dion and me to break up, she will inevitably place the blame on me again. My mother typically blames me when things don't go as planned, regardless of whether I am at fault or not. Just like last weekend, when my cousins were attacking me, she failed to defend me and instead shifted the blame onto me when I stood up for myself. It's an insult to my character.

Changing into a pair of gray sweatpants and a white tank top, I request an Uber to meet my therapist, Carol. I want to discuss my arrangement with Dion and the events involving my mother and cousins at the family dinner. I don't want to leave out any details, no matter how small, so that Carol can help me process everything and advise me on how to handle it. Dion is coming over after therapy to discuss the ins and outs of my family before we go to dinner. Scarlette will also join us since Skylar invited Darcy.

When I arrive at Carol's office, I take the seat closest to the hallway in the waiting room and scroll through Instagram. Skylar officially announced her engagement on social media. I know I should be happy for her, but I feel a twinge of jealousy at all the love she is receiving, even if *all* the praise isn't genuine. I learned the hard way that social media can be deceiving. After my breakup with Max, I deleted all of my pictures of us, and the women who used to comment heart emojis on our photos now pretend like I never existed. I even had to block some of them because Max gave the impression that I was a problematic Black woman…*whatever that meant.*

"Hello, Reign. Please follow me," Carol greets me, breaking my inner thoughts.

Carol's black heels click against the tiles, and her slim hips sway with each step of her pencil skirt as I trudge behind her down the hallway. We walk into her office, and she gestures for me to sit in the two-seater lounge chair while she grabs a binder with my name and date of birth. I sink into the chair as Carol sits across from me, flipping through the pages of the binder. She retrieves a pen and notepad and crosses her legs, looking up at me with a warm smile.

"So, how have you been feeling lately?"

My slumped shoulder is a dead giveaway of my distress.

Carol takes note of my body language, her pen poised to jot down any important details. "This is a safe space, Reign. Let's talk about what's been weighing on your mind," she says.

Steadying my nerves, I exhale a sharp breath. I feel humiliated opening up about my fake relationship with Dion; however, she is supposed to offer advice and never pass judgment. *Here goes nothing.*

"My sister recently announced her engagement to her short-term boyfriend."

Carol nods her head and scribbles into her notepad. "Congratulations are in order for your sister. How are you feeling about her news?"

"I'm happy for her, of course. Peter seems like a decent guy." Trying to find the right words, I pause for a moment before continuing. "But it's hard not to compare myself to her."

Carol listens attentively, encouraging me to delve deeper

into my feelings.

"I'm thirty-three years old and still single, and my mother never lets me forget it. My baby sister, who is not even twenty-five, is now marrying the man of her dreams after only knowing him for almost a year."

Carol leans forward, waiting for me to continue.

"When will it be my turn?" I let out an exasperated sigh. "I was pretty content with being single and focusing on my career after my last relationship. I was okay with my decision until my sister announced her engagement. Now I am the last single one in my family, and the pressure to find someone is at an all-time high." I search Carol's eyes for any signs of judgment, but I find none. She simply opens a water bottle and takes a sip.

"I…hired a fake boyfriend," I blurt out, and she chokes on her water, coughing slightly.

My eyes widen as she recovers.

She clears her throat and jots down some notes, nodding for me to continue.

"It's just for my sister's wedding, to get everyone off my back," I explain sheepishly. "My friend is beta testing her dating app, and there's a new feature that safely allows users to hire fake partners. I got paired with a guy named Dion James, and he's an actor. He, um, was in a peanut butter commercial when he was a kid." I shift nervously in my seat. "Uh, we hung out a few times and kissed once, but it's all fake." I pause, an afterthought crossing my mind, and I admit softly, "It's not entirely fake, actually. I think I might have feelings for him," I say, feeling embarrassed. "But I don't want to because I know it's not real, and he doesn't do relationships because of his profession. He'll also meet my parents tonight.

And… I'm going to stop talking now before I embarrass myself further."

Carol rips a piece of paper from her notepad and hands it to me. There is a circle drawn with the name *Mom* in it. The circle is surrounded by a bunch of other words, like *insecurities*, *marriage*, *money*, *wealth*, and *society*.

Unsure of what she's trying to convey, I look at her warily.

"Reign, let's talk about your mother."

My brows furrow in confusion. I talked a lot about my sister's engagement and hiring a fake boyfriend, and she wants to talk about my mother.

"Okay," I say slowly, "what about her?"

"Do you want to please your mother?"

"Why would you ask that?" I respond defensively.

Carol leans back in her chair, studying me intently. "Because it seems like everything you do is to seek her approval." I shift uncomfortably in my seat. "You were content with the possibility of spending the rest of your life single, but subconsciously, you feel like a disappointment to your mother because you haven't followed the traditional path she expected of you." She writes *Mom* on another piece of paper from her notepad, underlining it twice. "Tell me about your mother's reaction to your sister's engagement."

Feeling a knot form in my throat, I gulp. "Uh, my mother was overjoyed. Skylar is her golden child. Her and my cousins were raving about it at family dinner and making slick comments about me. My cousins told me I'm too old, no one wants me, and other hurtful things, and my mother shifted the blame onto me. I don't even know why I call her my mother. She's never been kind to me, and she's jealous of my relationship with my father."

"Were your cousins forced into the relationships they're in?"

Thinking about their husbands, I fidget with my hands on my lap. It seems like my aunt Shirl had a hand in arranging their marriages with eligible and wealthy suitors. However, I don't know for sure.

"I'm not certain if they were forced or not, but it seems like my aunt had some influence in their connections."

Carol tilts her head, her expression thoughtful. "Do you think your cousins are jealous of you?"

I burst out laughing at the thought. "Jealous of me? No way."

"Do they have jobs?"

I stop laughing and shake my head. "No."

"That could be a reason for jealousy. Sometimes you have to peel back the layers to see the truth," she remarks. "There are causes and effects to consider in every situation. Because of your sister's upcoming wedding—a cause—you are now in a fake relationship—an effect. And we will discuss your fake boyfriend in our next session." She glances at me, and I gulp nervously. "You are a successful and single woman—a cause. Your cousins may be jealous of your independence and career and that's why they make fun of you—an effect. Their way of coping may be to belittle you or make you feel inadequate." She flips through the binder in front of her, pausing on a page. "In one of our previous sessions, you mentioned that your mother and aunt were given an ultimatum to marry a doctor or a man with money—a cause. This might explain your mother's treatment of you. She projects her disapproval onto you for pursuing your own path and not following the expectations she has for you. Therefore, she treats you differently than she treats your sister—an effect."

My mind races as I connect the dots, realizing how deeply rooted these issues are.

"Your homework is to list all the positive and negative things your mother has said to you. We need to peel back the layers to understand her from within." Carol closes her notepad and opens up her calendar to schedule our next session. "Should we meet next week or keep it monthly?" She looks at me warily before adding, "I'd like to revisit our conversation about your aunt's husband in our next session."

My posture stiffens at the mention of my aunt's husband. "Let's meet next month."

Carol nods and writes down the appointment in her calendar. "In the meantime, work on that list and reflect on your relationship with your mother. We'll delve deeper into it when we meet again." With a reassuring smile, she closes her calendar and then places the binder back on the shelf, signaling the end of our session.

"Thank you so much for your time, Carol," I say as I gather my things and prepare to leave her office.

"It's my pleasure. Take care, and I'll see you next month," she replies as I walk out the door and request an Uber.

Chapter 13: Reign

Dion is on his way up, just as I am finishing up my makeup. The doorbell rings, and I quickly grab my notepad before heading to answer it.

I invite him inside and lead him to the living room, where we can discuss the rundown of my family before we leave for dinner.

"How's it going?" he asks, taking a seat on the sofa.

He's wearing a crisp white button-down shirt and dark jeans, looking effortlessly put-together.

My heart is pounding like a wild drum beneath my rib cage as I sit down beside him. "I'm doing okay," I reply, trying my best to contain my nerves.

He studies me. "Are you sure you're okay? You seem a bit tense."

Anxiety tightens in my stomach, coiling into a knot.

Rubbing my temples, I sigh heavily. "No, I'm not okay. My family… I don't know where to start."

He looks at me with an apologetic expression, his eyes softening. "Reign, I'd like to apologize again for what I said the other day. You were right. I knew what I was getting into when I agreed to be your fake boyfriend, and—"

Shaking my head, I cut him off. "It's okay, really. You have an honest and beautiful relationship with your parents, and I was being insensitive. You can tell them the truth."

"I was thinking of telling them we're just friends instead. We are friends, right?"

Feeling the knot in my stomach loosen, I smile softly. "I'd like to think we developed a nice *professionalship*."

He cocks his head, a hint of amusement in his eyes. "A what?"

"A *professionalship*," I say with conviction.

Dion chuckles. "Reign, that's not a real word."

"Well, it should be. It perfectly describes our situation."

"I guess it does," he concedes, a grin tugging at the corners of his lips.

After a comfortable silence, I break the quiet to start discussing my family. Opening my notepad, I flip through the pages.

"Here you go with this little notepad again," Dion teases, reaching over to peek at the scribbles.

I playfully shove him away. "Shut up! I like to be organized."

Chuckling and leaning back on the sofa, he says, "I know, I know."

A slight smile forms on my lips at his teasing before turning serious. "But on the real."

Dion smirks at my words. "On the real."

Squinting my eyes. "Yes, on the real, I want everything to go smoothly tonight. Our stories need to be straight so we don't slip up."

Dion nods in agreement, his expression turning sterner as well.

"We'll tell my family you're an underwear model."

Dion definitely has the build for it, he's so damn fine.

He raises an eyebrow, clearly amused. "An underwear model?"

"Yes, and we met in Central Park. You gave me your email address, and I sent you an email."

He laughs, raising his hands to stop me. "Wait, wait, wait. Email address?"

I glare at him. "What is so funny about that? I don't give my phone number to just anyone."

Dion chuckles, shaking his head. "Alright, alright. Email address it is," he says, playing along with the plan. "Then what? I patiently waited by the computer for you to email me?" He bursts out laughing, unable to contain himself.

I roll my eyes at his exaggerated reaction. "It's not that funny, Dion."

"Sorry, sorry," he says, his lips curling into a grin.

He is so annoying.

Shaking my head. "Anyways, I sent you an email after a week, and we met for lunch at a lovely French restaurant."

"The restaurant we had dinner at to talk business?" Dion asks, raising an eyebrow with a knowing look.

"Yes, that one," I confirm with a smile.

"Damn, you had me waiting a week by the computer for a date," Dion jokes, his eyes sparkling with amusement.

We lock eyes and burst into laughter, finding humor in the absurdity of the whole thing. When we finally calm down, we continue our conversation.

"Next on the list are my cousins: Raquel, Shonda, and

Robyn. Shonda is the oldest, Raquel is the middle child, and Robyn is the youngest. They are all married and supposedly working on having children soon. Their mother's name is Shirl, and she is my mom's older sister. Oh! And their father, AKA my aunt Shirl's husband is a retired doctor, he will be at the dinner as well."

Dion stops me and asks, "Why do you call him your aunt's *husband* and not your *uncle*?"

His innocent question causes my heart to sink like a stone in water. I do not respond right away, and his piercing gaze stays on me. A wave of unease washes over me as I struggle to find the right words to explain why my aunt's husband is not someone I consider family. The room feels still, and the air is thick. I can almost hear the deafening sound of my own heartbeat.

A crease forms between Dion's eyebrows as he looks at me. "Did I say something wrong?"

The weight of his question presses against my chest, and I struggle to find an excuse to avoid answering. How do I explain to him my resentment for a man who sexually assaulted me when I was a little girl? Instead of confronting him, divorcing him, and sending his sick ass to prison, my aunt chose to ignore the situation and pretend nothing happened. I have to smile through weekly family dinners, knowing what he did to me, while he completely ignores my presence.

"I don't want to talk about it," I finally manage to say, hoping to shut down the conversation.

Despite the worry etched on his face, he doesn't press further. Instead, he asks, "Is that everything?"

As I glance at my watch and notice the time, I quickly mention my parents. "I am very close with my dad, and I love him with all of my heart. My mother, on the other hand, is a bitch. Trust me, you will not like her."

His eyes are so big, they almost bulge out of his head.

Grabbing my purse, I smile. "Did I scare you?"

Dion composes himself, and a small smile forms on his lips. "I can handle a difficult mother-in-law."

"You've been warned," I say with a smirk as we head out the door.

Chapter 14: Dion

My eyes widen when we reach Reign's parents' lavish home. The grandeur of the estate blows me away. Only her mother and father live here, yet the house is enormous. Once I achieve my own success, I hope to buy a home as grand as this one for my parents as a token of my appreciation for everything they have selflessly done for me.

As we walk through the doors, a young woman greets us and takes our sweaters. Reign leads me to the kitchen, where the aroma of freshly baked desserts and finger foods wafts through the air. Another woman with dark hair and brown skin offers us a platter of fresh cheese.

"Would you like some cheese while you wait for dinner to be served?"

I nod in response, and she kindly hands me a saucer with a delicate piece of cheese.

"Would you like some bread to go with that?"

Nodding my head, I accept the offer for bread and she

brings over a warm loaf sliced perfectly for pairing with the cheese. I take a bite, and the creamy texture of the cheese melts in my mouth, complemented by the bread. I follow Reign towards the long wooden table set with elegant silverware and crystal glasses. As soon as we approach the table, everyone seated turns their heads in our direction, exchanging hushed whispers and curious glances. Sensing a growing uneasiness within me, I quickly consumed the rest of my cheese and bread.

"Reign, who is this stranger you've brought into our home?" A woman at the head of the table asks, her eyes narrowing. Her features are robust, and she exudes superiority. She looks a lot like Reign's sister, Skylar, so she must be Reign's mother.

Reign clears her throat and introduces me: "This is my boyfriend, Dion James."

Gasps and murmurs ripple through the room. Three women at the table, presumably her cousins, exchange disgusted looks while Darcy mutters something under her breath, causing Skylar to chuckle. Reign squeezes my hand and prompts me to take a seat next to her. The man sitting on the other side of her is most likely her father by the way they resemble one another.

He looks me up and down, his expression unreadable, before standing and extending his hand toward me. "Nice to meet you, young man. I'm Reign's father. It is a pleasure to have you here in our home."

I straighten up, returning his firm handshake. "Thank you for having me. You have a lovely place."

Reign's mother scrunches up her nose in disapproval, with a crease forming between her eyebrows. "We didn't invite you here. Reign, why did you bring this boy without asking us first?"

Reign shoots her mother a threatening glance, and I force myself to swallow the knot in my throat, trying to remain composed. I open my mouth to respond, but Reign beats me to it.

"I invited him, *Mother*. Don't be so rude," she says firmly, coming to my defense.

Her father clears his throat, diffusing the tension. "My lovely wife, let's not make a scene." He gives me a subtle nod, silently apologizing.

Scarlette enters the room and casts a wary glance at the table, assessing the awkward situation she just walked into. "Mr. and Mrs. Brown, family, Dion," she greets with a polite smile, taking a seat next to me. "I hope I'm not interrupting anything," she adds, trying to lighten the mood.

Grateful for a familiar face, I exhale a silent sigh of relief. Waiters and waitresses' bustle around the table, graciously pouring water to replenish our glasses. The atmosphere becomes more relaxed as everyone starts engaging in conversation, easing the tension that had previously filled the room. Reign squeezes my knee under the table. Her personality stands in stark contrast to her mother's, who appears pretentious and exhibits other negative traits. She's like a splinter stuck in your big toe that you can't seem to get out. It hurts a little, but it is more annoying than anything. Yep, that's her.

The waitress who previously served me cheese and bread returns with a platter of fresh salad and piping hot French onion soup. I lean over to Reign and whisper, "Do I eat the salad or soup?"

She giggles and whispers back, "Why not both? Anything you don't finish, they will take away."

"If I eat both, how will I have room for dinner?" I ask, feeling slightly overwhelmed by the amount of food in front of me.

Reign smiles, shrugging her shoulders as she reassures me, "You'll be fine."

The waitress places a plate of salad and a bowl of soup in front of me. Unable to recall which spoon to use, I discreetly glance at Reign and follow her lead, using the smaller oval spoon for the soup. Before I can finish my soup or salad, the entrée is served.

The aroma of the creamy tomato and spinach pasta makes my mouth water, and I wonder if I'll be able to finish it all. Reign catches my eye and gives me an encouraging nod. I take a bite of the pasta, and it's even more delicious than it smells.

I need the recipe for this dish!

Reign smiles at me, sensing my approval. "Are you enjoying your dinner?"

Nodding my head, my lips curve into a satisfied smile, and her lips mirror mine. There's some tomato sauce on the corner of her mouth, and I reach over to wipe it away with my napkin, causing her to blush slightly. *Damn, she's so beautiful!*

Her cheeks are a rosy shade that complements her brown skin, and there's a warmth in my chest as I gaze at her.

Reign breaks the moment by saying, "After dinner, we will go to the living room for dessert, where I will formally introduce you to everyone."

I thought she already introduced me.

After what seemed like years, it was dessert time, and Reign and I walk together with our arms entwined. The family is already conversing, and Reign makes a gesture toward the man standing next to Skylar. I follow her gaze.

"That's my sister's fiancé," she whispers, her brown eyes sparkling with amusement. "His name is Peter Peterson."

We both chuckle quietly. "Why did his parents do that to him?"

"Who knows?" she says, stifling a laugh as she glances over at two women. A tall, brown-skinned woman with short, curly black hair, and a lighter-skinned woman with long black hair. "Those are my cousins Raquel and her husband, Allan, and Shonda and her husband, Ronald. Ronald never says anything. He just sort of stands there like a statue of Frankenstein," she explains, peering over to her mother next, who is engaged in conversation. "The dark, brown-skinned woman talking with my mother is my other cousin, Robyn. She wears way too much makeup. Her foundation doesn't even match her neck," she whispers, rolling her eyes. "Like, girl, how do you have a dark-brown skin tone on your neck but super light brown on your face? At least have your makeup match," she chuckles under her breath.

"Well, sheesh!" I laugh along with her. "So, these women are your cousins, huh?" I ask, keeping my voice low.

Reign sighs and responds, "Yeah, they are my bitchy cousins." She gestures to another woman across the room who appears uninterested in anything other than herself. "That's my aunt Shirl and her husband."

I notice how her body tenses when she mentions her aunt's husband, but I don't press, instead taking in the scene before us. I brace myself for what's to come as we make our way further into the living room.

As the room falls silent, all eyes turn to us, and Reign whispers, "Just smile and nod."

Trying to fit in with the rest of the family, who are clearly scrutinizing us, I mimic Reign's every move—smiling and nodding. Darcy rolls her eyes at us, and Skylar doesn't seem to notice our presence at all. *I don't know what her problem is.* Her soon-to-be husband, on the other hand, gives me a slight nod, which I return. Reign's cousins' husbands don't even acknowledge us, and Reign's mother directs a disapproving glance our way.

Reign clears her throat, drawing more attention to herself. "Hello, everyone. I would like to officially introduce you to my boyfriend, Dion."

Smiling nervously as their collective gazes turn to me, I prepare myself for the inevitable questions and judgments that are sure to follow.

"Why would anyone want to date her?" Raquel whispers loud enough for me to hear, and the other two women beside her snicker.

I usually don't like to call women out of their names, but those three fit *the word* that Reign uses to describe them perfectly. Reign reaches for my hand, and I entwine my fingers with hers.

"What do you do for work?" Reign's mother asks.

I take a deep breath, ready to face their scrutiny. "I am an underwear model."

Scarlette giggles as I answer while Reign sends a warning glance in her direction.

"How did you meet my daughter?" Reign's father asks, his gaze stern.

Reign's preparation for this dinner equipped me with well-rehearsed responses.

"We met at Central Park," I say smoothly, gazing into Reign's eyes. "I knew I wanted to get to know her better from the moment I saw her."

Reign squeezes my hand in response, a small smile playing on her lips. Little does she know, I mean every word that I am saying.

She is the most beautiful woman I have ever met, inside and out. I do want to know everything about her; however, we have this arrangement that complicates things. I want to tell her the truth about my developing feelings, but I'm not sure how she will react. What if she doesn't feel the same way, and this is strictly business for her? She's paying me to do a job, and I feel like I am doing well. Still, falling for her was not part of the plan. *Wait?* Am I falling in love with a woman I barely know? That only happens in movies and books, right? It doesn't happen in real life!

"She gave me her email address, and after about a week, we finally went on a lunch date and have been inseparable ever since," I continue, planting a soft kiss on her cheek.

"I don't know why anyone would be attracted to someone like Reign," Shonda remarks, a disgusted look plastered on her face.

Shonda's disapproval only fuels my feelings for Reign even more. Gently biting down on my bottom lip and feeling the slight pressure of her hand on mine, I meet Reign's gaze.

True love doesn't always follow a script.

Relishing the warmth and smoothness of her skin, I lift Reign's chin and raise an eyebrow to signal her that I'm about to lean in for a kiss. Our lips draw closer, the anticipation filling the air with a gentle electric buzz. As our lips draw dangerously close, the words flow effortlessly from my mouth. "Anyone with eyes can see how beautiful Reign Brown is," I respond, feeling more confident than ever about my feelings for her.

The refreshing scent of her delicate perfume excites my senses as I press my lips against hers, savoring the softness and sweet taste of her mouth. The air around us is filled with the faint sound of our breaths, along with gasps and whispers. As our lips finally meet, a surge of passion courses through me and rush to my throbbing dick. Reign responds with equal enthusiasm, her hands reaching my chest, deepening the kiss. A calm silence surrounds us as we lose ourselves in the moment.

Reign's mother sneers and makes a face of utter disgust, unable to hide her contempt. "That is enough PDA in my house," she scolds and turns away to her sister to engage in conversation.

We pull away, cheeks flushed and hearts racing.

In contrast, Reign's father nods in approval before joining his wife in conversation. Shonda's face remains shocked while the other two turn their noses up toward us. Scarlette grins, visibly entertained by the situation, and strolls away to the side with Skylar, Peter, and Darcy.

"Oh my gosh!" Reign whispers, still catching her breath. "I can't believe we just did that." I trail behind her as she heads to the kitchen. "Did you see Shonda's face?" she asks, a giggle escaping her lips.

I chuckle in response. "She looked like she saw a ghost," I reply, sharing in Reign's amusement as we continue to relive the moment in hushed tones.

She shakes her head in disbelief. "I don't think I've ever seen her that flustered before."

"I take it that I did not disappoint," I say with a grin, feeling a sense of accomplishment.

Reign nods enthusiastically, her eyes sparkling. She jumps on me and wraps her legs around my waist. "You did amazing," she says, catching me off guard by pressing her lips against mine in a passionate kiss.

My eyebrows shoot up in surprise, and I return the kiss. However, she suddenly breaks away, disentangling herself from me with a nervous laugh. "I'm so sorry. That was a… thank you kiss," she stammers, blushing furiously.

I miss her touch immediately and wish she hadn't pulled away so fast. "No need to apologize," I assure her, reaching out to gently touch her cheek. "It was my pleasure."

A blush tinges on her cheeks, and her lips tremble as she looks up at me.

The desire I have for her is unlike anything I've ever experienced before. She enthralls me in a way I never thought possible. Her presence ignites a fire within me. The sweet sound of her voice stirs my soul.

The burden of upholding this agreement has become too heavy for me to bear.

I can no longer keep up this charade.

"Reign, I have to tell you something."

Her eyes widen in anticipation, her breath catching in her throat as she waits for my words.

"I—"

Darcy walks in on us, interrupting the moment.

She glances between us. "Um, Reign, Sky wants to discuss your progress on planning her wedding."

Reign rolls her eyes. "Can it wait?" she asks, her attention still focused on me. "We have plenty of time until the wedding. Dion and I are in the middle of something."

Darcy looks me up and down. "I'm sure whatever you two are doing can wait. Your sister needs you now," she says.

Reign sighs, shooting me an apologetic look before excusing herself to deal with her sister's request. I'm left standing there, the weight of my unspoken words heavy on my chest. My shoulders sag. I might have missed my chance to tell Reign how I feel about her.

Chapter 15: Dion

As I wait for Reign to return to the kitchen, a server approaches me with a tray of drinks, which I eagerly grab and toss back.

With a sense of urgency, Reign walks over toward me, her brows furrowed and a worried expression on her face, Scarlette following closely behind.

"We have to go. Now!" she says.

Before I can ask what happened, I see her mom, aunt, and cousins rushing over to greet someone.

"It's too late," Scarlette says in a defeated tone.

"Who is that?" I ask, trying to see what all the fuss is about.

Reign doesn't say a word as she loops her fingers with mine. Following her lead, we make our way back to the living room area, where the rest of the crowd is.

A man is standing in the center of the room, embracing Reign's family members.

When our gazes meet, I realize I know him.

"Mr. Johnson," I shout over the chitter chatter.

"Coach James," he exclaims, his eyes wide and a bead of

sweat forming on his forehead. "W-what are you doing here?" he stammers.

The room fills with a collective gasp in surprise.

"Wait…you two know each other?" Scarlette asks.

Reign's eyes search mine, waiting for a response.

Who is Mr. Johnson to Reign?

"Uh yeah, we know each other."

Mr. Johnson's eyes are vast, and he is subtly shaking his head *no*.

"His son is on the little league team that I co-coach with my friend Eddie."

Mr. Johnson's shoulders droop and he lets out a deep sigh, bringing his hand to his forehead.

Reign's breath quickens and it is as if she sees nothing but red. "How old are the kids on your team?"

Not understanding the switch in her emotions. "Are you okay, Reign?"

"Dion, answer my question!" she shouts.

"They are between fourteen and fifteen years old."

Scarlette covers her mouth and the rest of the room falls silent.

Mr. Johnson rubs the back of his neck.

Reign descends into uncontrollable laughter, and I'm unsure what is so funny. She's the only person in the room laughing, and everyone is looking at her, confused, including myself.

"Reign, is everything okay? I don't understand—"

Reign waves her hand, cutting me off. "Dion, this is my ex-boyfriend Max from seven years ago. You said the kids on your team are between the ages of fourteen and fifteen, right?"

Nodding my head in response, I attempt to reply; she holds her hand in front of my mouth. "I'm not finished. Which means this asshole piece of shit had a kid while we were together!"

My face drops as she turns to Mr. Johnson or, instead, *Max*—her ex-boyfriend. "You are a fucking asshole; not only were you cheating on me, but whoever that poor child's mother is—" She stops and shakes her head, directing her gaze toward her mother. "And you—you have always invited this asshole—this *cheater* to every event. Never taking my side."

Everyone in the room is in shock, and there is so much tension that you can cut it with a knife.

Reign throws her hands in the air. "Fuck this!" she barks, grabbing her things and walking out the door, leaving everyone else at a standstill.

"My apologies," I say, nodding my head and hurrying behind her.

Reign is walking extremely fast, and although shorter than me, I find myself trying to catch up with her. *I didn't know this evening would end like this.*

"Reign," I call out, trying to get her to slow down.

Reign is speed-walking as if a thief is hot on her heels, desperate to steal something of value.

"Reign, can you please slow down?" I call out to her once more, my voice echoing in the distance.

When I catch up to her, she turns around and falls into my arms, sobbing. *How could he cheat on someone as kind and beautiful as Reign?* I want to rush back into her parent's home and punch him in the face.

"Reign, I'm sorry."

She looks up at me, a waterfall of tears streaming from her face. Inhaling her intoxicating vanilla scent, I hold her tight, wishing I could take away all of her pain. Reign pulls away slightly, wiping the tears staining her cheeks with the back of her hand. She takes a deep breath and then reaches for her phone to request an Uber. "I must look like a mess right now."

I shake my head, "You look beautiful, as always."

A glimmer of a smile forms on her face as she looks up at me. "Thank you for saying that," she sniffs, her eyes still glistening with tears.

Closing the distance between us, I place her head on my heart and trace circles on her back. We stay this way until the Uber arrives.

A heavy ache settles in my chest as I see her fragile figure fade away into the car. Her shoulders drooped, and her face streaked with tears.

Friday

June 7ᵗʰ, 2024

Chapter 16: Reign

I cannot believe that Max had a child the entire time we were together. *How could he hide something so significant from me?* I always thought he was an asshole, but this… this is a new level of betrayal. It has taken me years to get over him, and now it feels like my heart is breaking all over again—not because I have feelings for him but because he lived a double life and I never knew it. What a fucking prick! *I need to do something to get my mind off his dumbass!*

A cold shiver runs down my spine as the thought of Dion crosses my mind. The memory of our eyes locking, him gently pulling me closer, and the sensation of his soft lips meeting mine is still with me. I replay that moment along with the priceless expressions on my cousin's faces.

The anticipation of seeing him again is driving me crazy. However, we don't have any scheduled meet-ups planned. Maybe I should text him? *No, you shouldn't.* My inner voice shouts! Even if I am starting to feel something for Dion, it's not going to work out. I hired him to be my boyfriend and after what happened with that asshole, how can I trust another man with my heart? What if Dion is just as bad? He is acting, and he's doing a great job at it.

Shaking the thought away, I try busying myself with planning Skylar's wedding instead, yet my thoughts keep drifting back to that unforgettable kiss. And then, when I jumped on him in the kitchen, he caught me and kissed me back with equal passion. That couldn't have been acting; we were alone in the kitchen. Perhaps he refrained from pulling away because he didn't want to hurt my feelings. Still, the intensity of that kiss felt undeniably real. It left me wanting more, craving him in a way I never expected. It was unlike anything I had ever experienced before. There was something inside of me that I never knew existed, and he awakened it.

Maybe there's a chance for something more between us.

I grab my phone from the nightstand and send him a message.

I hasten to the bathroom to shower and change before heading out to meet Dion. He lives in Freeport, so it will take me some time to get there. I rush out of the door and take the elevator, my mind still distracted by our kiss. I can't tell if he feels the same way I do, because we have a signed contract. I pay him monthly by check, and he has been depositing the payments into his account. Still, if he didn't feel the same way, he wouldn't meet with me outside of our scheduled events, right? Or what if I'm reading too much into it? If I admit my newfound feelings to him and he rejects them or, worse, laughs at them, things could get awkward. That would be humiliating!

Pull yourself together!

We are in a *professionalship*. This is just a business relationship, not a *romantic* one. Rather than inviting Dion to every social event, I will only ask him to do the ones required for Skylar's wedding; however, I intend to invite him to accompany me to Ms. Daniels' wedding as my plus one.

When I reach the rec center, there's a group of guys exiting with towels around their necks and sweat-soaked shirts. I walk past them and head straight to the front desk to check in and pay. The girl at the front desk directs me to the women's locker room to access the gym.

I tread through the locker room and down the narrow hallway, the sound of my sneakers bouncing off the walls. As I enter the gym, I notice Dion right away, his thick arms glistening with sweat.

He catches my eye and approaches me with a smile as his friends leave the gym, shooting me sly smirks that make me uneasy. *I wonder what he told them about us.*

Dion taunts, "Are you ready to lose?"

Shoving him playfully, I make a face. "Why do you assume I'm going to lose?"

He shrugs, his lips curling into a confident grin, revealing his signature dimple. "You're right, I haven't seen you play yet."

He leads me to the basketball court, and I drop my bag on the side and start stretching.

His brows furrow in amusement as he watches me.

"What's so funny?"

"Nothing," he replies, his grin widening.

As I pause my stretching routine, I direct a questioning look towards him. "Seriously, Dion."

He chuckles and says, "I just find it cool that you stretch before playing. The dudes I play with never do that."

Rolling my eyes. "Well, I'm not a dude."

He chuckles again, his dimple deepening. "I can see that."

I resume stretching, feeling his eyes on me as I warm up.

"Those are some nice basketball sneakers," he comments with a smirk.

A crease forms between my eyebrows as I glance down at my feet. "Are you mocking me?"

Dion laughs, holding up his hands in defense. "Nah, not at all."

"Yeah, sure, whatever!" I stand up and grab the ball from the ground. "My ball first. Are we playing to seven or eleven?"

He shrugs, still smirking. "Let's make it seven."

"I'm going to kick your ass." I stick my tongue out at him like a teenage girl, dribbling the ball onto the court.

His smirk widens. "After I kick yours, let's get something to eat."

My breath catches in my throat. *I have something you can*

eat. Swallowing hard, I push down the dirty thought that popped into my head and regain my focus.

"We are playing by one's and two's," I say, trying to sound nonchalant. "And loser pays for lunch."

If I can manage to score from the three-point line, I will earn two points, whereas scoring from within the three-point line or inside will only earn me a point.

He nods, a smirk lingering on his lips.

"Check." I signal the start of the game and throw the ball to him.

He throws the ball back to me with a competitive glint in his eyes, matching my own. The smooth leather of the ball feels familiar in my hands as I charge towards the basket. He frowns in concentration as he tries to block my shot; however, I sink the ball into the net with a satisfying swish.

"One to zero," I call out, a triumphant grin spreading across my face.

"Just getting warmed up," he shoots back, his competitive spirit shining through.

"Check," I taunt as I pass him the ball.

He catches it effortlessly, and I brace myself for his next move. He dribbles towards me, his focus unwavering. I steal the ball from him with a quick crossover and create space for a midrange jump shot. *Swish.*

"Two to zero," I boast, bouncing my shoulders in victory.

Dion screws up his face and removes his shirt, throwing it to the side. His rippling muscles make my mouth water. I want to run my fingers along his abs, but I quickly return my focus to the game. His gaze locks onto mine, determination burning in his eyes. This time, he plays a tighter defense. Before I can dribble the ball, he knocks it out of my hands, drives it to the basket, and scores with a layup. *That was so sexy!*

"Two to one. Check," he says, his confidence restored. He throws the ball back to me, ready for the next round.

As the game progresses, Dion posts up on me several times, taking advantage of his height and strength, and he shoots a fadeaway, resulting in a four-to-two score. He tries to defend against me again and shoots another fadeaway, but my hand brushes against his abs, disrupting his shot and causing the ball to miss. I know that was a foul, and I hesitate for a couple of seconds for him to call it; however, he doesn't, and I go in for the rebound, take the ball, and shoot the jump shot.

"All net!" I exclaim as the ball swishes through the hoop. After recovering the ball, I shoot from behind the two-point line without dribbling, sinking another shot. "Point game!"

He is playing tight defense, so I fake left and go to my right, making a layup.

"Game!" I fist pump in the air.

Dion looks impressed as he concedes defeat. He compliments, "Okay, okay, you're good," his lips curl into a sexy smile.

I smile back. "Thanks. I played basketball in junior high and high school."

He picks his shirt up from the side and wipes the sweat from his forehead. "You still got it."

"You're not too bad yourself," I reply, playfully shoving him.

He gulps down his water bottle, then wipes his mouth with the back of his hand. I'm fixated on his lips, envisioning all the ways they could be put to use.

"Reign?" He calls my name, snapping me out of my

thoughts. "You ready to go?"

Trying to dismiss my provocative thoughts, I nod. "Yeah, let's go. Want to come over to my place?"

"Lunch is on me," he says, flashing me a charming smile. "What do you feel like eating?"

I wish you would eat me.

My heart flutters at the thought. "How about some sushi?"

He wrinkles his nose, and I laugh. "Don't knock it until you try it."

We get back to my place, and I head straight to the shower first, leaving Dion to unwind on the balcony. As I step under the warm water, I think about how much fun I had playing basketball with him. I haven't played in months, and it felt good to be back on the court, especially with him. I lean against the tiled wall, remembering how his left dimple appeared when he made back-to-back shots and how his face tensed when I made mine. What's stopping me from telling him how much I enjoy our time together? Maybe I should go for it and see how it goes, but if he doesn't reciprocate, I'm not sure I can handle the rejection. It's a risk I'm not ready to take just yet. Still, the thought of not knowing how he feels is weighing on me.

Stepping out of the shower, I dry off and dress in something comfortable. I meet Dion in the living room and hand him a towel and washcloth, trying to act casual despite my internal turmoil. He thanks me with his signature smile and heads to the bathroom to freshen up. As he disappears behind the bathroom door, the thought of joining him crosses my mind, but I quickly push it away, not wanting to complicate things further. Instead, I distract myself with the sushi menu. I absentmindedly browse through the options, trying to focus on something other than the sound of running water from the bathroom and the image of Dion's sexy ass body standing there, dripping wet. I can only imagine his erect member bobbing up and down in the water. Shaking the dirty thought away, I finally settle on my usual California and Ebi Tempura rolls.

Dion joins me back in the kitchen, leaning against the counter with his shirt draped over his shoulder. "I never had sushi before. What are you ordering?"

Why is this man so damn fine?

Dion pulls his shirt over his head. He doesn't even realize how wet he is making me right now. I just want to straddle him on the floor and ride him until we're both breathless.

"Reign?"

I glance up, meeting his gaze, and a blush creeps up my cheeks. "Yes?"

"What are you ordering?" he repeats, his eyebrows knitted together.

"Um, just the California and Ebi Tempura Rolls," I reply, trying to sound casual despite the butterflies in my stomach. "The California roll has avocado, crab meat, and cucumber in it, wrapped in seaweed and sushi rice. And the Ebi Tempura roll has fried shrimp, avocado, and radish sprouts inside, also wrapped in seaweed and sushi rice. They're both really good."

Dion screws up his face, and I laugh at his expression, feeling a bit more at ease now that we're discussing food.

"Trust me, it's delicious!"

He shrugs, giving in. "Okay, Reign, I trust your judgment," he says, finally relaxing and flashing me a sexy grin that sends shivers up my arms, down my legs and straight to my aching clit.

We move to the balcony while we wait for our food to be delivered. The evening breeze rustles through the air as we settle into the comfortable lounge chairs, and the bustling city fades into the background.

I exhale a sharp breath, and Dion studies me with a curious expression, as if trying to decipher my thoughts.

"I was wondering if you would like to accompany me to a wedding."

His brows shoot up. "Uh, sure. Whose wedding is it?"

"It's a work thing. I attend all the weddings I plan," I explain nervously, watching his expression shift to one of interest. "I thought it would be nice to finally have a date for one of these events."

His lips twitch into a grin, and I quickly add, "I also need an assistant because my sister is only interested in her own wedding and not the other clients, so it's double the work. I would pay you extra."

His grin widens. "I'd be happy to help out. Don't worry about the pay."

My eyes widen like saucers at his generosity, and a vast smile spreads across my face. I can almost kiss him in that moment, but I hold back and simply say, "Thank you so much, Dion! I really appreciate it."

He chuckles and replies, "No problem at all."

A knock at the door diverts our attention to the arrival of our food. The moment I am greeted by the irresistible aroma of freshly prepared sushi, I can't help but lick my lips. I carefully arrange the sushi on two plates and carry them back to the balcony, where Dion eagerly awaits.

He takes the plate from me with a grateful nod. "When is the wedding?"

"It's on Thursday, June 27ᵗʰ, at 7:00 p.m., but we need to arrive by 4:00 p.m."

He nods, and I watch him fumbling with his chopsticks before taking a bite of the California roll. He chews thoughtfully, savoring the flavors. His lips curl into a smile as he looks up at me.

"See," I say, nudging him with my elbow. "It's good, right?"

He laughs. "Yeah, it's really good."

"Try the Ebi Tempura next. It's my favorite," I suggest, pointing to it on his plate.

He picks it up and takes a bite, his eyes lighting up in delight. "Wow, this is amazing!"

I smile, taking a sip of my green tea. "When we finish eating, do you want to go to this little boutique down the street to browse for matching outfits for the wedding?"

Dion stops chewing and grins.

"What's so funny?" I ask, narrowing my eyes. "I don't mean like we're going to wear the same thing, just coordinating colors."

Chuckling and shaking his head, he responds, "I know what you mean."

"Is that a yes?" I press.

"Sure, why not?" Dion responds with a shrug.

"I'd also like to thank you again for what you did in front of my cousins. I don't think I can ever thank you enough. The looks on their faces were priceless. I also wanted to apologize for my reaction to Max, it's just he—"

Dion interrupts me, brushing his hand across my cheek. "Reign, it's okay, and of course, I was happy to do it. Anything for my girlfriend."

A warm flush spreads across my cheeks as I choke back a

gasp.

He quickly corrects himself. "My pretend girlfriend."

My heart sinks at the clarification, and he looks away, concentrating on his sushi. I pick up my chopsticks and focus on mine as well.

As we eat in silence, I can't help but wonder if there's a deeper connection between us.

Chapter 17: Dion

Today's weather is perfect for a stroll—sunny but not too hot. While walking to the boutique with Reign, I admire her natural beauty and wonder if she has any idea of the effect she has on me. The way she played ball earlier was a turn-on, and maybe, just maybe, there could be something real between us. Still, what if I'm misreading the signs and she's just being extra friendly? And if she is interested, am I prepared to be in a committed relationship? I have been single for this long because I don't have much to bring to the table. Let's face it: I'm broke, and I can't offer her the kind of lifestyle she deserves, so why bother pursuing something that may not work out in the end?

Reign's gaze meets mine, her eyes sparkling with joy and a hint of something more. "We're here."

We enter the quiet little store, and a friendly sales associate greets us. "Welcome to Layla's Boutique."

Reign smiles back at her before turning to me. "Would you like to choose an outfit first? There's a men's section on the left with a variety of formal attire and a women's section on the right with cocktail dresses, pantsuits, and an abundance of heels."

You would think Reign works here. Shrugging my shoulders, she grabs my arm and leads me towards the men's section.

"The bride decided on a Valentine's Day masquerade as the theme of the wedding at the last minute."

I grin a little. "Which part was last minute? The Valentine's Day theme in June or the masquerade part?"

Reign lets out an exasperated sigh, browsing through the racks of suits. "The masquerade part. She literally decided on it two weeks ago, and I have been running around like a crazy person trying to get everything together in time. I haven't even had time to go to my therapy session."

She selects a dark gray slim-fit dress pants from the rack and hands it to me. "I think these will look great on you." Reign tiptoes to find a matching dress shirt for the pants. "Since it's Valentine's theme, I was thinking we could go with red. What do you think about this shirt?" She holds up a red button-up shirt.

Nodding, I take the shirt from her. "Sure, I trust your judgment."

She grins and flags down a sales associate for the fitting room.

A dark brown-skinned woman approaches us and directs us to an available one. As I try on the outfit, Reign waits outside. I step out and see her eyes light up with approval.

She holds up a black mask, winking suggestively. "This will complete the look."

Taking the mask from her, I chuckle and strut to the podium. Checking myself out in the mirror, I adjust my collar and secure the mask in place.

Reign walks around me, taking in the outfit from all angles and smoothing out any wrinkles. "You're going to turn heads in this," she nods in satisfaction, a smile forming on her plump lips.

My lips curl into a grin. "Your turn."

"Oh, yeah! I already know what dress I want to wear," she exclaims. "I'll be right back."

With a twirl, she disappears, and I notice the other women in the store casting flirty glances at me when she's out of sight. Stepping off the podium, I find a seat and scroll through my phone while waiting for Reign to return.

She appears a few minutes later, cradling a sparkling red dress in her arms. "Wait right here," she says, disappearing into the fitting room to try it on.

Patiently waiting for her to emerge from behind the closed door, I scroll through my phone again. When Reign comes out of the room, my jaw drops to my toes. The dress fit her like a glove, accentuating her curves and making her look good enough to eat. *Fuck! I just want to taste her.* I want to take her back to my dressing room, lay her down and dip my head between those sexy thighs, and feast on that pussy until she screams my name.

Reign twirls around, a smile spreading across her face as she catches my reaction. "What do you think?"

You look so damn good! I just want to fuck you into next week!

Reign stares at me with a blank expression. "Dion?"

Closing the distance between us, I try to clear my thoughts before responding, "You look beautiful, Reign. Just stunning."

The intensity of my gaze makes her cheeks flush as she looks down shyly. "Thank you, Dion," she replies.

Nearly losing control, I hold my breath, reaching out to stroke her sweet lips gently; however, Reign interrupts by placing a black and red feathered mask over her face.

"I almost forgot the final touch," she says.

We lock eyes in the mirror, and the saleswoman claps her hands in approval. "You two make a splendid couple," she says.

Reign steps down off of the podium, and I scratch the back of my neck awkwardly. I reach my hand out to take hers, and our gazes lock in a silent understanding. *This is my only chance to tell her how I feel.*

"Reign, I have to tell you something," I mumble.

She looks at me expectantly; however, her phone rings, interrupting the moment.

"Sorry, it's Skylar. I have to take this," she says apologetically before stepping away.

Not again!

"Wait, Reign!" I call out, trying to hold her back.

She closes the door behind her before I can say another word. My shoulders slump in defeat. Every time I work up enough courage to tell her how I feel, something always seems to get in the way.

It's like the universe is conspiring against me.

She opens the door, peering out with her phone resting on her shoulder. "Skylar is going to the wedding. Do you still want to come with me?"

"Sure," I reply, retreating to my fitting room to change back into my clothes.

Her phone is still on her ear when I emerge, and she looks up at me. "I'll see you on June 27th for the wedding."

"I will see you then," I reply with a slight smile.

She kisses me on the cheek, which sends blood rushing straight to my manhood before heading out the door with her phone up to her ear.

Wednesday
June 26th, 2024

After lunch with my parents and hearing them go on and on about their trip, I stop by Eddie's to get a game of 2K.

"Hey bro, how's it going?" He gives me a fist pound as I walk into his one-bedroom bachelor pad.

Grabbing a controller and sitting on the sofa. "I just had lunch with my parents. Now I need a game to relax and unwind."

Eddie turns on the console and hands me a cold beer. "How is your mom doing? How's your dad? And what's been going on with you?"

Taking a refreshing swig of my beer, I respond, "They are both doing well. They just got back from the Bahamas. And nothing much has been going on with me."

I told Eddie about Mr. Johnson—*Max*—being Reign's ex-boyfriend without going into much detail about Reign's reaction to the news.

"Did your parents ask about your 'professionalship' with Reign?" Eddie asks, gesturing quotation marks.

My parents did ask about Reign, but as she suggested, I told them that we were costars. Which, in a way, we are.

"Bro, that's not even a word," I reply, laughing.

Eddie grins, focused on the screen, as he picks his team. "Reign says it is, so it is."

I select my team and adjust my defense while Eddie mindlessly scrolls through his phone.

"Bro, are you done yet? Why do you be taking so long?" He asks impatiently, glancing up from his phone.

"Listen, let me do my thing," I reply with a smirk. "I'm almost done. Patience is a virtue."

Eddie sucks his teeth and leans back on the sofa, taking a sip of his beer.

He clears his throat to speak. However, I know he's about to ask about Reign, so I cut him off.

"Don't start."

He raises his hands in surrender. "Just hear me out for a second."

Furrowing my brows. "Fine, make it quick," I say, pausing the game and placing the controller on the table.

He smirks. "How about you tell Reign how you feel tomorrow after the wedding or at some point during it?"

Inhaling and exhaling slowly. "I'm telling you, something always comes up when I'm about to tell her how I feel. It's like the universe doesn't want me to confess my feelings."

Eddie gives me a disapproving look. "I think you're scared and using that shit as an excuse to avoid telling her how you feel. Stop making excuses and just do it."

"If I tell her that I want to pursue her for real and she doesn't feel the same, then I'm going to look like a fool!"

"Dude, so what? We are not in college anymore. We are pushing forty, and life is too short. Just tell her how you feel, or I will."

His bluntness strikes a chord. "How is that not a college move?"

Eddie shrugs. "I don't know, man. Maybe it is. Still, I think Reign is attracted to you, too. You just have to make the first move."

Raising an eyebrow. "How do you know that?"

He nervously scratches the back of his neck. "Well...I've been meaning to tell you something." He pauses, clearing his throat. "Scarlette and I have been hanging out."

My eyes are vast, and I shake my head in disbelief. "You and Scarlette? Does Reign know?"

Eddie nods, a sheepish grin on his face. "Reign doesn't know…yet. And Scarlette is a cool girl, and she's so hot."

I give him a playful punch on the arm, smirking. "Well, good for you, bro. Don't mess it up."

He chuckles nervously. "I'll try not to."

A brief silence falls between us before I speak up again. "Did Scarlette say something about Reign being into me?"

His grin fades slightly. "Uh, not in so many words."

"What did she say exactly?" I press.

Eddie stares at the TV screen, avoiding eye contact.

"Eddie?"

Finally, he looks back at me and says, "She just asked if you had real feelings for Reign."

"Why would she ask that?" I frown, and a crease forms on my forehead. "What did you tell her?"

He shifts uncomfortably before responding. "I told her I didn't know, and it's not my place to say."

Nodding slowly. "One moment you say either I tell her or you will, and the next you say it's not your place to say."

Eddie chugs the rest of his beer before answering, "You are a grown-ass man, Dion. Start acting like one."

"Man, whatever. I will tell her when I'm ready." I mutter under my breath, unpausing the game.

"Suit yourself. Don't come crying to me when she's in the arms of someone else."

Eddie hits a nerve with his comment, and I quit the game to avoid losing my cool. "She hired me to be her boyfriend. Having genuine feelings for her is not part of the job description, Eddie. And what makes you think she will even believe that I do want to be with her?"

"Actions speak louder than words. Maybe if you stop

depositing the checks, she'll realize that your feelings are more than just an act."

His suggestion is so ridiculous that I can't help but scoff at it. Still, he may be right.

"I didn't deposit the last check yet, and I guess I won't deposit the next ones either. I will find another way to come up with the money for the uniforms."

Eddie grins knowingly and claps me on the back. "Oh yeah, that's right. If anything, bro, I got you. What else is stopping you from telling her the truth?"

"Bro, I can't let you do that. It's my turn to provide the uniforms."

Eddie and I co-coach a summer league team in our community; we provide these kids with a positive outlet and keep them away from trouble. It doesn't start until the middle of July, so I have some time to save some money. Coach Jimmy began the league and hand-selected Eddie and me to continue it. I feel like it's my way of giving back to my community.

"Dion dude, how about we just go half?"

"Okay, cool. I will pay you back, though."

Eddie shrugs. "No worries, now what is it? Don't dodge the question."

I take a deep breath and exhale slowly, letting all the tension leave my body. "She's so out of my league, man. What makes you think she would ever go for a guy like me? I'm broke and an unemployed actor."

My shoulders slump, weighed down by the burden of my failures and insecurities.

What chance do I have with someone like her?

"None of that shit matters. If she's into you, she won't care about any of that. It will be who you are as a man that will win her over, not what you have or don't have. I don't think Reign is a shallow woman—she's independent. Anything she wants, she can get on her own, so stop focusing on your shortcomings."

"I should be able to provide for my woman as a man, though," I mutter.

Still, Eddie's words start to sink in. My focus is usually on the big picture, causing me to overlook the more minor details that matter in a relationship. Before I can think about anything else, I need to tell her how I feel. Everything else can come later.

Sucking in the air, I straighten my shoulders. "I'm going to tell her tomorrow," I say.

"Good for you, man," Eddie encourages, throwing me the controller.

Chapter 18: Dion

I put on my red button-up shirt and dark gray fitted dress pants, making sure I look sharp for the occasion, and then I request an Uber to take me to the venue. Reign and I are meeting at 4 p.m. to allow enough time to ensure a smooth ceremony and reception.

As the Uber pulls up to the curb, I check my watch and realize I have a few minutes to spare. Reign is already waiting outside, looking even more stunning than she did when she first wore the sparkling red dress. She delicately styled her luscious curls into a high bun, complemented by a silver diamond-crusted headband and loose curls framing her face. Reign completed her look with a pair of pearl earrings and a matching necklace. As she greets me with a warm smile, her silver stilettoes click against the pavement, and her breasts gently rise and fall with each breath. Her presence is enough to make my mouth water and my cock shudder.

"Hi, Dion," she says, her voice like music to my ears.

"Hi, Reign. You look beautiful," I say, unable to tear my gaze away from her striking appearance.

"Thank you," she replies, a hint of blush coloring her cheeks as she takes a step closer. "You don't look half bad yourself."

She tilts her head, and our eyes lock, a silent understanding passing between the two of us.

"Follow me," she says, leading me into the venue. "We have work to do before the ceremony starts."

Catching a whiff of her sweet vanilla perfume, I walk closely behind her. We take the elevator to the third floor, where the event is being held. The space is decorated with red and black accents. A prop-filled photo booth stands in the corner, a large screen displays a slideshow of the couple, and a path of rose petals leads to the bride and groom's table.

Reign walks over to her assistant, Nancy. "Please list everything that has been completed and what remains."

Two women and a man enter, carrying centerpieces filled with red and black roses.

"Please place these on each table," Reign instructs the brown-haired woman standing beside her, holding the centerpiece.

I admire Reign in her natural element. Her eyes gleam with fulfillment and purpose as she oversees every detail of the event, conveying her pride in her work.

Skylar walks in with a woman, pointing around the room. Our gazes meet, and her lips form a thin line. "Hello Dion, nice to see you again."

Oh, she speaks! I really don't know what her deal is.

Nodding politely in response. "Nice to see you too, Skylar."

She nods her head and walks off to the side with the

woman she came with.

So, I guess she's not assisting with preparations.

Turning my attention to Reign and Nancy. "Reign, is there anything I can help with?"

She looks up at me, relief evident in her eyes. "Actually, yes. Can you assist with arranging the centerpieces on the tables? Since my sister is not helping." She rolls her eyes at Skylar, who is now seated at a table, laughing with the woman.

"I'll take care of the centerpieces," I assure her.

Grabbing the arrangements from the pushcart, I start placing them on the tables. A man walks over to Reign with a frown on his face, and I overhear him mention that there is no MC for the reception.

Reign looks flustered as she checks her phone, and it is as if smoke is pouring out of her ears.

I step in; however, she waves me off. "I need a moment," she tells me firmly, storming out of the room.

Skylar looks over her shoulder at the commotion and then resumes her conversation with the woman. *Useless!*

Following Reign out of the room, I catch up to her in the hallway. She is pacing back and forth, muttering to herself, and when I approach her, she wipes away a single tear that had escaped down her cheek. I steady her shoulders, and she takes a deep breath, exhaling slowly, and looks up at me.

"Dion, I don't know what to do! And Skylar isn't helping at all," she says, her voice trembling with frustration. The anger overwhelms her, and more tears well up in her eyes, staining her cheeks.

"Take deep breaths and try to calm down," I say, wrapping my arms around her.

She pushes me away, shaking her head, "I can't calm down,

not when there is no MC! You may not understand this. An MC is crucial for the success of a reception!"

"How about I do it?"

"You? But you're not a professional MC," she scoffs. "Do you even know what an MC does?"

"Uh, no, not exactly," I admit, feeling a bit ashamed.

She narrows her eyes at me, clearly unimpressed. "I can't believe this shit! And Skylar is such a bitch! She's supposed to be helping me; however, she's chatting with that woman instead of doing her job. I love my sister, but what the fuck! Ever since she announced her stupid engagement, she hasn't been any help at all!" Reign shouts in frustration, throwing her hands up.

Her eyes are filled with unshed tears that compel me to offer comfort and support. "I may not be a professional; however, I'm an actor. Just tell me what I need to do, and I will do it. Are there lines? What does the MC need to do?"

"Introduce the wedding party."

"I can do that. I just need a script." I grasp Reign's shoulders, meeting her gaze. "Reign, I can do this for you."

Her tense shoulders relax slightly, and Nancy interrupts us with sheets of paper in her hands. "The maid of honor gave this to me."

I quickly glance at the papers and see that they're the names of the wedding party. Reign is about to say something, but I hold up a hand to stop her. "I've got this," I assure her, taking the papers from Nancy and scanning them.

"The ceremony starts in twenty minutes. We need you downstairs, Reign," a man calls out from behind us.

Reign nods at the man and then turns to me with a look of panic on her tear-streaked face. "I am depending on you,

Dion."

Nodding back at her, I wipe away a stray tear on her cheek. "I got you, Reign. I promise."

She straightens her posture and smooths down her dress before taking a deep breath and rushing to the elevator with Nancy. Looking back at me once more, she mouths a quick "thank you" before disappearing.

I familiarize myself with the names of the bridal party. *I will not let Reign down.*

The ceremony and reception went well, and afterward; I helped Reign drop off some supplies at her boutique. Skylar's new assistant turns out to be the same woman she's been talking to all night, and to my surprise, she helped bring some of the boxes inside. I don't understand why Skylar has an assistant when neither she nor her assistant helped Reign or Nancy during their crisis.

I cannot believe Reign has been dealing with this the entire time.

Reign places a box on the shelf, turning to me with a tired smile. "Thank you, Dion," she says gratefully. "I appreciate all of your help today."

Patting myself on the back, I smile back at her. "Thank you, thank you. I told you all I needed was a script."

Her lips curl into a genuine smile as she snakes her arms around my neck, and I rest my hands on her waist. "You're a lifesaver," she whispers, increasing my heart rate. "I owe you one."

Our embrace lingers for a beat, both of us smiling at each other in a silent understanding.

My eyes drop to her lips, and I hold back from leaning in to kiss her. Instead, I slightly pull away and say, "Reign, I have something to tell—"

"Me first," she cuts me off, closing the gap between us by pressing her lips against mine.

It's unexpected, but I reciprocate, savoring the feeling of her soft lips against mine. I lift her off the floor and onto her desk, nestling between her parted legs as the world fades away around us. She doesn't pull away, her body leaning closer as she deepens the kiss. The soft sound of her moans fills the air, intertwining with the delicate brushes of our lips. My fingers trace lightly along her inner thigh, and a shiver of anticipation runs through me. We behave with untamed passion, our lips locked, our hands exploring, our tongues teasing, and our mouths tasting. My hand slides up her dress, feeling the dampness on her silk panties as she reacts by arching her back. I know in that moment that I never want this to end; I want to savor every second of it until reality comes crashing back in.

The room brims with a tense stillness, only broken by the hushed rustling of our bodies that send shivers down my spine. Just as we are about to surrender to our desires, the sudden entry of Skylar shatters the moment. The sight of her wide eyes and the sound of her gasp freezes us in place, leaving an uneasy tension hanging in the air.

Reign pushes me away, her cheeks flushed with embarrassment, and quickly straightens her dress.

Attempting to play it off, I give Skylar a sheepish smile.

"Sorry, we were just..." I start to explain, and Skylar cuts me off with a quick shake of her head.

"Don't stop on my account," she says, closing the door behind her.

Unsure of what to do next, I look at Reign for guidance. She avoids my gaze as she fidgets with the hem of her dress. Feeling the awkward tension between us, I wonder how this will affect our arrangement. I clear my throat, trying to think of something to say to break the silence, and Reign's expression changes from discomfort to disgust.

"I am so sorry, Dion. That was very unprofessional of me," she says, finally meeting my eyes with a look of regret.

"What? No, it's okay, Reign."

She shakes her head, her eyes filled with shame. "No, it's not okay. I am paying you. I–I don't know what got into me."

I reach out to gently touch her arm. "Reign, I kissed you back. I wanted to kiss you. And I still—"

Pulling back, she interrupts me. "No, Dion. This can't happen again. I think you should go."

"But I—"

"Please, just go," she pleads, avoiding my gaze. "I need to be alone right now."

I try to touch her arm again, but she firmly shakes her head. "Please, Dion. Just go," she repeats in a low tone.

My heart sinks to the floor and I turn my back and begin to walk away.

Thursday
August 8th, 2024

Chapter 19: Reign

I'*m standing in front of the mirror, admiring my reflection and assessing my appearance. My dress fits me like it was tailored specifically for my body, hugging my curves in all the right places. Dion appears behind me, wrapping his arms around my waist as my heart flutters.*

His warm breath tickles my neck as he whispers, "Baby, as beautiful as you look in that dress, I want to rip it off of you right now."

I gasp, feeling his arousal press against me as his fingers skillfully trace a path up my dress.

"Do you want to take it off, or should I help you with that?" he asks.

Butterflies swarm in my stomach as our eyes meet in the reflection of the mirror.

Exposing my neck, I sweep my hair to the side and lean into his touch. He slides down the zipper on my dress, igniting a fire within me that only he can quench.

As the dress falls to the floor, he whispers in my ear, "You're even more beautiful without it."

His words cause shivers to travel down my spine, and he turns me around to face him, firmly pushing me against the wall. He explores my body, his fingers stimulating me through the delicate lace of my underwear. My mouth parts in anticipation as he pushes my underwear to the side, his gaze never leaving mine. He gently slides a finger inside me, then another, until three of his fingers are skillfully moving in and out of me. As waves of pleasure wash over me, I moan.

Leaning against the wall for support, I relish in the sensation of his touch, feeling myself getting closer and closer to the edge. My body arches instinctively towards him, silently begging for more, but Dion suddenly stops and withdraws his fingers from inside me.

I whimper in protest, my eyes pleading with him to continue.

"Not yet." He sucks on each of his fingers, tasting my essence while staring directly into my eyes.

His fingers are against my inner thighs again, sending shockwaves throughout my body. Dion's intense gaze assures me that there is more pleasure to come.

My breath comes in short gasps, the sound echoing in the quiet room as I anxiously wait for him to continue.

"I want you to come for me, baby," he whispers huskily.

A moan escapes me as his fingers are finally inside me again.

Dion rubs his thumb in circles over my clit while penetrating me with his fingers until I'm on the brink of release. As I reach my peak, my breath catches in my throat, and I release a passionate cry while waves of pleasure course through my body.

Beep-beep-beep.

The sound of my alarm clock wakes me up from my sex dream about Dion. I groan in frustration, wishing I could go back to sleep and continue where the dream left off, but reality beckons. I haven't seen Dion since the wedding, and to be honest, I'm embarrassed. He texted me a few times to talk about that night; however, I never responded. I don't know how I feel about it. He kissed me back with equal passion like he felt the same way I do. Was it just a spur-of-the-moment thing, or is there something more between us? Falling for him wasn't part of our deal.

How can I trust my feelings when they seem to be leading me astray?

How can I trust Dion?

Max broke my heart into a million little pieces when we were dating, and although I was past the cheating, hurt, and pain, it all came rushing back to me the moment I found out he had a son the entire time we were together.

How do I know that Dion won't hurt me as well?

He's been wanting to talk about it; however, I've been avoiding the conversation.

Today is Dion's birthday; perhaps I should send him a happy birthday text to keep things amicable.

Other than that, I need to put all of my attention toward my sister's wedding and my work.

I'm not ready to face him yet.

Three dots appear on my screen, then disappear. They appear once more and then disappear again. *What is he going to say?*

Suddenly, my phone rings, causing me to jump, and I hit the ignore button. *Shit!* He's going to know I hit ignore on purpose. *Reign, you are acting like a child!* My inner voice shouts.

I don't know if I can hear Dion's voice right now.

Maybe he was caught up in the moment when I kissed him.

Our kiss could have a different meaning for me than it did for him. He's an actor and knows how to play a role.

I'm spiraling right now. Maybe I should call him back.

I take a deep breath and hit the call button. He picks up on the first ring. *Damn, that was fast.*

Dion: "Reign, how are you feeling?"

Me: "I am fine, Dion. H-how are you?"

Dion: "When can I see you again?"

Exhaling once again, I bite my bottom lip; I want to see him. I want to explore whatever this is that we have developing, but I just can't.

Me: "Dion, I-I think we should remain professional."

Dion: "Reign, I really want to see you so I can speak to you. What I need to say must be done in person."

Me: "Dion, look, I think we need to stick to our business agreement."

Dion: "Reign, listen to me."

Me: "No, Dion. I will see you for my sister's rehearsal dinner. I agree that we need to talk; however, I think it would be best to stick to the agreement and discuss whatever is happening between us afterward."

Dion takes a deep breath over the phone and mumbles something under his breath.

Me: "Dion?"

Dion: "Y-yeah, sure, Reign. We will talk then. Take

care."

He says, hanging up the phone before I can say another word.

It's been a while since I've seen my therapist because of work and my sister's upcoming wedding, so I dragged myself out of bed for my 1 p.m. therapy session. Skylar has not been helpful with wedding planning or preparations for our clients. She is the epitome of a Bridezilla bitch, and I'm so over it. I'll be interviewing candidates over the next few weeks in the hopes of finding someone to fill her position. At least, when Skylar is gone, she will no longer be occupying space at my boutique. Nancy has been accommodating, and I plan to give her a raise when I can afford it.

Running through my morning routine, I dress in my favorite gray sweatpants and white T-shirt, grab a quick breakfast bar, and head out the door.

I stride into Carol's workplace for my therapy session and take a seat in the waiting room. Once I am settled and scrolling through my phone, I remember I was supposed to make a list of all the good things my mother had ever said to me and the negative comments she has made. The problem with that is my mother has mainly said cruel things to me. Opening my notes app, I limit myself to the top five.

"Hi Reign, Carol is ready to see you in her office now," the receptionist informs me.

"Thank you," I respond, making my way to her office.

"Hello, Reign. It's nice to see you again," Carol greets me with a warm smile as I take a seat across from her.

"Hi, Carol. Nice to see you, too."

She flips through the pages of her binder. "It's been so long since our last session. Why is that?"

I've been so focused on work and everything else I have going on that I haven't gotten around to reschedule my appointment. Luckily, she has agreed to see me today.

My shoulders droop slightly. "I've just been really busy with work and planning for my sister's wedding, and..." I trail off, wondering if I should mention Dion.

"And?"

"Where do I even begin?" I sigh.

Carol opens her notepad and reads through her notes from our previous session. "I tasked you with writing down the good and bad things your mother has said to you. Would you like to start there, or would you like to discuss your fake relationship? Or your uncle?"

My body tense up at the mention of my aunt's husband.

"Let's start with my mother." Scrolling through my notes, I let out a frustrated sigh. "My mother has never said anything nice to me. She has said plenty of hurtful things, though. She told me that I was useless and a liar. She said no man in his right mind would want to marry me because I am too old. She told me I was the reason my ex cheated on me and that I would never find true love because no man wants to be with a woman who is too independent. Oh! And she told me I'd never be as good a daughter as Skylar. And that's just naming a few. I don't know why I was cursed to have her as my mother! Some girls are like best friends with their mothers, but I will never have that kind of relationship with mine." I roll my eyes and fold my arms like a teenage girl.

"The only reason I *love* her is because she gave birth to me. But that's about it."

Carol studies my body language, jotting down notes as she listens to my frustrations. "It sounds like you've reverted to a little girl who just wants to please her mother," she observes, offering a new perspective. "I believe your mother has some childhood trauma of her own that she has never fully dealt with, and instead of confronting it, she has projected her unresolved issues onto you. Some of the things she has said to you perhaps her mother have said them to her. Your mother is perpetuating the cycle with you. The difference is that you have done well for yourself, not depending on a man for your success like she did." Carol flips through her notebook as she continues, "Why did you hire a fake boyfriend?"

Fidgeting with my hands, I shift uncomfortably in my seat. "I needed a date for my sister's wedding," I admit quietly, but it sounds like a weak excuse.

"Why? You seemed satisfied being single after your last relationship ended."

"I know, but my family doesn't see it that way. I didn't want them talking about me being dateless again, especially at my sister's wedding."

"You wanted to please your mother."

A crease forms between my brows. "I'm sorry?"

"You were content being single. Then your sister announced her engagement, and she is the favorite child. Therefore, you hired a fake boyfriend to please your mother or to get under her skin."

A knot forms in my stomach. Carol has a way of getting me

to admit things I don't want to.

I didn't want my cousins to judge me for not having a date for yet another wedding, and the way Shonda's mouth dropped open when Dion kissed me lives on in my mind.

"Maybe it was a bit of both. Having a boyfriend has been the talk of the family, taking some of the attention away from her favorite daughter's wedding. And if I'm being honest, it felt good to see their faces when I walked in with Dion. My only issue right now, or one of them, is that I have real feelings for Dion, but I'm not sure if he feels the same way. I kissed him, which was unplanned; however, he didn't pull away, and he kissed me back. Maybe he has feelings for me, too."

Carol listens intently to my rambling.

"Still, I'm not sure because he's an actor. I also don't trust him completely yet. How can I? Given his profession, it blurs the lines between reality and acting. And to make matters more complicated, he knows Max. Oh, and how could I forget. The reason why Dion knows him is because Max had a son the entire time we were together. And Max's son is on Dion's little league team he coaches in the summer."

"Reign, you have to let go of the hurt and pain from your previous relationship in order to see this one through fresh eyes. If Dion shares your feelings, then you need to give him a fair chance. Actors have real emotions, just like everyone else. You need to talk to him openly and honestly, and if he doesn't feel the same for you, then that's okay. You are a strong woman, and you will pick up the pieces and move on, just like you always have. And when you're ready to start dating for real, not because you're under pressure but because you want to, you will be able to approach it with a clear mind and an open heart."

Using the back of my hand to brush away a stray tear. "I want to wait until after Sky's wedding or honeymoon to talk to him."

Carol smiles sympathetically, passing me a tissue. "That sounds like a good plan." She waits for me to compose myself before adding, "Do you have a contract?"

Nodding my head. "Yes, my lawyer drafted an agreement for him to pretend to be my boyfriend until the day of my sister's wedding, during which I would have paid him $10,000. Everything is in writing, and I keep copies of the checks for my record."

She nods. "That seems like a fair arrangement." Carol shifts in her seat, crossing her legs. "Let's backtrack to your mother and cousins. The little girl in you is desperate to prove to them that their assumptions about you are wrong. You need to tell little Reign that you got this and that she can take a step back."

Releasing a deep breath, I nod in understanding, fiddling with my cuticles.

"Before our meeting today, I made bullet points outlining what I wanted to discuss with you. We talked about your mom, cousins, and Dion. Now, let's move on to your uncle."

"You mean my aunt's husband?" I snap back.

She calmly responds, "Yes, your aunt's husband. Are you ready to tell me what happened? You mentioned he touched you inappropriately in one of our previous sessions."

My heart races as I recount the painful memories.

"However, every time I try to bring it up again, you shut down."

My nails are digging into my palms, and I exhale a sharp breath. "I already worked through my feelings about it on my own."

Carol narrows her eyes, leaning forward in her chair. "Are you sure, Reign?"

Trying to maintain eye contact, I nod. "Yes, I'm sure."

Carol studies me for a moment before leaning back in her chair, her expression unreadable. "I don't believe you've fully dealt with the trauma. It's important to address these feelings to heal."

A lump forms in my throat as I realize that perhaps I haven't fully processed what happened as much as I thought.

When I open my mouth to respond, my mind floods with memories and emotions that I've been avoiding. "Every other weekend when I was a little girl, I would spend the night at my cousin's house. One night, when the girls were sleeping, I went to the bathroom to pee. He walked in on me, but instead of leaving or apologizing, he stood there and watched me, telling me to wipe myself slowly. I didn't realize how wrong it was so I never told anyone. I didn't want to sleep over there anymore, though; however, I was pretty much forced to keep going there because my mother didn't want to be bothered with me, and my dad was working. That disgusting man touched me a few times when we were alone. I eventually told my mother and aunt about what had happened, but they didn't believe me and accused me of lying for attention. They had no choice but to listen to me when I threatened to go to the police, but they swore me to secrecy."

Tears stream down my cheeks as I recount the painful memories. "My father still doesn't know what happened to me."

Carol looks at me with sympathy in her eyes. "I'm so sorry you had to go through that when you were just a little girl."

I hate that man, but it happened over twenty years ago, and

I don't have any proof. If I ever have children, they will not be allowed to sleep over at anyone's house.

"I don't call him my uncle, and it doesn't matter anymore. Besides, he doesn't say anything to me or acknowledge me, so it's whatever," I say dismissively, trying to convince her or, better yet, myself that I am, in fact, okay. I know that I'm not okay, but admitting it out loud is too painful.

Carol remains silent for a moment before gently saying, "It's okay to not be okay. You don't have to pretend that everything is fine all the time. Family is supposed to protect you, and yours has failed you." She closes her notebook before continuing, "Today's session was a good start, but I believe there is more here, and you can tell me when you're ready. For your homework, I want you to think about every traumatic event in your life that you have overcome."

I furrow my eyebrows in confusion and ask, "How will reopening old wounds help me?"

Carol smiles softly. "It's all part of the healing process. Trust me."

A slight smile tugs at the corners of my mouth. "Trust the process," I repeat silently to myself.

As we wrap up the session, she jots down a few more notes and looks up at me. "Will I see you in a month, or..." she trails off.

"I will call you to schedule our next appointment. I have so much going on," I say, standing up and gathering my things.

"No worries, Reign. I am just a phone call away."

I thank her for her time and head out the door. While I am walking, I stop at a nearby bench and pull out my notebook to begin working on the homework Carol assigned to me. As I start writing, the weight of my family trauma and the pain of my ex's betrayal hit me hard. A waterfall of tears stream down my face. Carol is right about Dion, she's right about everything. If he feels the same way about me, I need to give him a fair chance and see him through a different lens.

I'll have this conversation with him after Skylar's wedding.

Thursday
October 24th, 2024

Chapter 20: Reign

I haven't seen Dion since June. I wonder how he's been doing since we last spoke. I've honestly been avoiding him like the plague. Today is my sister's wedding rehearsal and birthday, and I'm getting ready; however, my stomach is in knots thinking about the upcoming conversation with him. I left my door unlocked because he should be here soon, and my heart is pounding against my ribs. Although we agreed to talk after my sister's wedding, I intend to tell Dion about my feelings when he arrives, hoping that he feels the same way. It's time to just rip the Band-Aid off because I haven't been able to get that kiss out of my mind.

There is a light knock on my room door, and I take a deep breath as Dion lets himself in, looking just as handsome as I remember. A lingering scent of sandalwood, warm and slightly spicy, fills the air as he approaches me.

Dion wears a black tuxedo, highlighting his muscles and the bulge of his crotch, and he holds a single black rose. His eyes meet mine, and there's an undeniable attraction that makes my palms sweat.

I want to push him on to my bed, rip this dress off of me and ride him like a wild woman. As he approaches, he hands me the black rose, and I accept it with a shaky hand. He then reaches into his pocket and pulls out a small velvet box, opening it to reveal a beautiful rose gold necklace. My breath catches in my throat as he places it around my neck.

"Reign," he says my name with a softness that sends shivers down my spine, "I've been wanting to tell you something."

Ready to finally lay my heart on the line, I take a deep breath and he closes the distance between us, his hand reaching out to touch my cheek.

My breathing quickens with eagerness. "What is it?" I manage to whisper, my voice barely audible.

His eyes lock with mine, filled with longing and uncertainty. "I want you, Reign. I want you more than anything I've ever wanted before."

My heart skips a beat at his confession. "Do you only want to fuck me, or do you want to be with me, too?"

Dion gently brushes his thumb against my cheek. "I want it all, Reign."

Just when I thought my heart couldn't swell any further, he takes out his wallet from his back pocket, pulls out the checks from June till now, and rips them to shreds before my eyes. My hands instinctively flies to my cheeks in shock.

I didn't realize he hadn't cashed any of the checks since June.

"Reign, I want you to let me love you and fuck you in ways you have never experienced. I want to make passionate love to you, eat that pussy, and make you come more times than you can count. My sweet rose, I want to be with you in all ways. I'm done pretending."

Is this really happening? I pinch my arm to make sure I'm not dreaming.

"I wanted to tell you for months, but every time I worked up the courage, we were interrupted, and then you kissed me that night in June, and you've been avoiding me ever since."

I look away. This feels surreal, but his words are crystal clear.

He places his finger under my chin, gently guiding my gaze back to his. "Please say something, Reign."

Instead of speaking, I take action and lead him to my bed. I leap on top of him, ready to give him all of me. I kiss him with a passionate urgency that I didn't know I had in me. He responds eagerly, wrapping his arms around me as if he never wants to let go. Our quickened breaths and racing hearts fill the room.

"I want you too," I say in between kisses.

"Do you only want to fuck me, or do you want to be with me, too?" He asks, his lips curling into a sexy smirk against my lips.

I pull back slightly and stand to my feet to unzip my dress. He restrains my hands, looking deep into my eyes. "Are you sure?"

"Yes," I assure him with unwavering certainty.

He releases my hands and lets me continue undressing. My dress fall to my ankles as I step out of it, and his eyes pool with desire. He follows suit, shedding his own clothing. My eyes light up with delight as they feast upon his well-defined abs, muscular thighs, and sizeable hard dick peeking through his boxers. *Damn, he is so fine!*

"Not that I don't want to," he says, his voice husky, "but what about your sister's wedding rehearsal dinner?"

"Fuck that," I reply, removing my bra and panties and tossing them aside. "I want you inside me now."

He doesn't need to be told twice, as he removes his boxers. His hard member springs up and my mouth nearly falls open at how big he is. *Damn!* I push him back onto the bed, straddling him.

"Shit, I don't have a condom," he says, his hands gripping my hips.

I nibble his earlobe and whisper, "I'm on the pill and we are both clean."

A groan escapes his lips as I slowly lower myself onto him. When he is all the way in, I moan. It's been so long since I've had sex that I almost forget how good it feels.

"Are you okay?" he asks softly, his hands caressing my back.

My eyes locked with his, I nod. Adjusting to his size and length, I slowly move up and down on him.

"Fuck," he mutters, his fingers digging into my skin as our bodies move in perfect harmony, the pleasure building between us with each thrust. "You are so fucking wet," he grunts, guiding my movements.

As I ride him, he rubs his thumb over my swollen clit and I throw my head back in pleasure. My body shudders when I reach my climax and he removes his thumb. He leans toward my neck, his hot breath tingling my skin. My grip tightens on his shoulders, and I bite down on my lip to stifle a moan. He then captures my lips in a passionate kiss. I taste him, savoring his familiar lips and the way they move against mine. Our heavy breaths mingle as we lose ourselves in the moment. Dion takes control and flips me onto my back, heightening my anticipation. His eyes darken with a primal hunger, and he thrusts his fingers inside me, rippling shocks of pleasure through me—my back arches involuntarily as he expertly brings me to the brink of ecstasy once more. I gasp for air, my body trembling.

"You like that?" He whispers huskily in my ear.

Unable to form words, I nod. He withdraws his fingers and replaces them with his erect member, increasing his pace as he plunges deeper into me. Our intertwined moans echo through the room. Dion stimulates my clit, sending me spiraling into a frenzy, the sensation pushing me closer to the pinnacle of my release. I grip him tightly, my nails digging into his back. With each movement, I feel myself teetering on the edge, the intensity building with every thrust. Dion's movements become more urgent, driving me towards a climax that I can no longer hold back. With a few final thrusts, I shatter into a million pieces, my body convulsing with ecstasy as Dion follows closely behind, both of us collapsing in a state of blissful exhaustion. My body feels weak from the multiple orgasms I have experienced.

The room is infused with the scent of our passion as we lay intertwined, basking in the afterglow of our shared intimacy.

We show up at my sister's dinner an hour late. Scarlette and Eddie greet us outside when we arrive, their smiles widening as they see the contented look on our faces.

Eddie fist bumps Dion, and Scarlette exchanges a knowing glance with me, wriggling her eyebrows suggestively.

"What did we miss?" I ask as Dion snakes his arm around my waist, planting a kiss on my cheek.

Scarlette giggles and says, "Just Sky and Peter's entrance, their speech, and the bridal party lineups. But I'm sure you two had a good reason for missing it."

I playfully roll my eyes at her. "I'm sure she didn't even notice. She's been so self-absorbed with her wedding."

They all laugh as we make our way to the dining hall. Eddie and Scarlette link arms and walk ahead of us, while Dion squeezes my waist, pulling me closer to him, I feel his dick rub against my ass through our clothing and all I can think about is getting home for another round with him. I sneak a glance at him and catch his smirk. I know he's thinking the same thing because he presses his lips to mine and whispers, "I'm ready when you are."

As we enter the room, my mother approaches us with knitted brows, closely followed by my father.

"Where were you? You missed your sister's entrance and speech. Darcy had to step in for you."

"Sorry, there was traffic on the way here." I lie, looking past her and smiling at my father. "Hi, Daddy. I'm sorry, Dion and I are late."

My mother's posture remains stiff, and she narrows her eyes at me. My father simply nods in understanding before pulling me into a hug and shaking Dion's hand. "Nice to see you again, young man."

My mother rolls her eyes at me as the bridal party is seated for my sister's dinner, and she storms off, leaving my father trailing behind her.

Darcy approaches us next, her arms folded across her chest, and I internally roll my eyes at her obvious disapproval.

"You're Skylar's wedding planner, but you're late, and I've been handling everything in your absence."

"And you're doing a great job," I say, giving her a pat on the head.

Darcy huffs, calling me a bitch under her breath.

I raise an eyebrow at her; then I turn to Dion, who is watching the exchange with a raised eyebrow of his own. He pulls me close to him in a protective manner, and we walk past Darcy. I don't even bother responding because I'm in such a good mood that no one, not even my mother, can bring me down. Darcy can handle the rest on her own. She's the maid of honor. I've already done more than enough to ensure Skylar's wedding goes smoothly.

I'm here as a guest.

Chapter 21: Dion

Reign Brown is finally mine, and I couldn't be happier. After Skylar's dinner, we returned to Reign's place and made love over and over again until the early hours of the morning. The fact that both of us had gone without sex for an extended period of time made it even more significant.

Skylar and Peter exchanged vows, and now it is time for the cocktail hour.

As the cocktail hour progresses and we mingle with the other guests, Reign and I can't take our eyes away from each other. My gaze flickers back and forth to my watch, as if I can magically move time forward with sheer willpower.

I grip Reign's waist and whisper, "I can't wait to get out of here and have my way with you."

Reign leans in closer, her lips grazing my earlobe as she murmurs, "You have no idea how much I want that too."

Her breath quickens as she pulls away slightly, motioning towards the exit. I follow her lead, the sound of our hurried footsteps echoing in the empty hallway as we head to a more secluded spot where we can finally be alone. We find ourselves in a dimly lit stairwell, and she pins me against the wall, her eyes filled with hunger that matches mine.

I reach out to delicately tuck a loose curl behind her ear, and she leans into my touch, her lips parting slightly as she closes the distance between us. After months of anticipation, when our lips finally touch, everything else fades away, leaving only our electric connection. Our bodies press together, fitting perfectly like two pieces of a puzzle, as we lose ourselves in the passion of the moment. I want to fuck Reign against the wall right here and now, then take her to bed and make love to her all night long. Savoring every inch of her skin and every sound she makes until the sun rises, and we are both exhausted and completely satisfied.

"We should leave after they cut the cake," she says against my lips.

I squeeze her ass in my hand, feeling her smile against my mouth. "I'm ready to leave now."

She laughs, her hand lowering to my crotch as she whispers, "I can tell."

My lips curl into a smirk as I shrug my shoulders.

Reign gently rubs the bulge in my pants, and I let out a low groan. "You have to fix that before we walk back inside," she teases before pulling away and straightening her dress.

I pull her back toward me, pressing my dick against her ass. "The only way to fix this is for me to be inside that wet pussy," I whisper in her ear, my voice husky with desire.

She moans, her body arching into mine. "There will be time for that later," she breathes. "Let's just get through cocktail hour and the reception."

I groan, reluctantly releasing her and adjusting myself

before following her back inside. We mingle with the other guests, exchanging pleasantries and sneaking glances at each other when we think no one is looking. The expectation of what's to come later only heightens the hunger between us.

When cocktail hour concludes, we are seated at the table farthest to the right of the room, not too close to the DJ but not too far. I've never been to a Halloween-themed wedding before, and the decorations are impressively festive. I was expecting ghosts, spiders, webs, and all things Halloween. Instead, the room is adorned with elegant black and orange accents, pumpkins, and flickering candles. Platters of marshmallows and chocolate-covered strawberries, delicately glazed with orange frosting, are placed around the centerpieces. It seemed more fall-themed than Halloween.

The bridesmaids are wearing black strapless dresses with orange belts. Reign explained that she was not a part of the wedding party because she was planning the wedding. She was relieved not to have the added stress of being a bridesmaid and she also commented on their unflattering dresses. Skylar, in an off-white dress complemented with vibrant orange and black accessories, stood out among the bridesmaids, *as she should*. Her groom, Peter, wore a classic black tuxedo with an orange boutonniere, which Reign had explained to me what a boutonniere was because I had no idea. They're a perfect match for each other.

Shaking Peter's hand and hugging Skylar, I congratulate them. To my surprise, she thanks me. She seems to be less tense now that the wedding planning is over.

Reign is currently engaged in conversation with Scarlette, so I join Eddie at the bar.

"Are you enjoying the festivities?" I ask, ordering a drink

for myself.

"Yeah, it's cool," he replies, taking a sip of his drink. "So, you and Reign, huh?"

I grin, clinking my glass against his. "Yeah, man."

"My man," Eddie says proudly. "You finally told her how you feel."

"Yeah, I took your advice and ripped the checks up in front of her, and the rest is history," I say with a smile.

I watch Reign on the dance floor with Scarlette and August. She is a sight to behold, and I'm so happy she is mine.

"I'm happy for you, bro. I have never seen you this whipped before," Eddie chuckles.

"I know, man. But she completes me. You know she can play ball?" I brag, proud of her skills on the court, just as she, Scarlette, August, and her husband Calvin join us.

"I can what?" She asks with a playful smile.

"You heard me."

She places her hand over her ear. "No, I didn't hear you clearly. Say it again."

"You can play ball," I repeat proudly.

"Oh yeah, I can," she says, bouncing her shoulders up and down as she did when we played.

"Although you cheated when you brushed your hand along my stomach."

Reign playfully rolls her eyes at me.

"Don't think I didn't notice," I raise a brow.

Eddie and Scarlette watch in amusement as we banter back and forth.

"You two are cute," he chuckles.

"I love you two together." August adds as Calvin nods his head in agreement.

I stop bantering with Reign and look deeply into her beautiful brown eyes. "That's what sealed the deal for me. Reign Amara Brown, I knew from that moment I wanted to be with you."

A smile slowly spreads across her face. Time seems to pause, and it feels like there is no one else in the room but us.

"De nada," Scarlette says, breaking the moment with her trademark humor.

Eddie laughs and shakes his head.

"Excuse me?" I say.

"Well, if it wasn't for my app, you two wouldn't be together." She says, flipping her hair back with a playful grin.

August and Calvin exchange confused glances.

"Later," Scarlette says, waving her hand toward them.

"And I guess if it wasn't for me pushing you to finally tell her how you feel, you two wouldn't be together either," Eddie jokes, nudging me with his elbow.

Reign and I share a knowing smile.

"You're right. Thank you, Scarlette, for setting me up with the most beautiful woman I've ever met," I say sincerely. Reign blushes, averting her eyes shyly. "And thank you, Eddie, for convincing me to make a move."

Scarlette and Eddie exchange a proud look, clearly pleased with their matchmaking success. We continue to enjoy the evening until Darcy's commanding presence draws everyone's attention, signaling that it is time to cut the cake.

Reign and I lock eyes, a silent understanding passing between us. She breaks eye contact first to walk to Skylar and Peter's table, and I follow closely behind. She whispers something in Skylar's ear, eliciting a gasp and an eager nod from her.

Skylar winks at me, and I nervously scratch the back of my neck.

"What did you say to her?" I ask Reign, trying to hide my curiosity.

She smirks mischievously and replies, "I told her we were leaving to go get it in."

I burst out laughing. "You are not serious?!"

She grabs my hand, hastening us out of there. "Dead serious," she says with a laugh. "Let's go!"

Chapter 22: Dion

We can't keep our hands off each other as we make our way out of the elevator to Reign's penthouse door. My tongue on her neck causes her to fumble with her keys, but she quickly recovers and unlocks the door. As soon as we step inside, she pushes me against the door with a sense of urgency, her lips meeting mine in a fiery, passionate kiss. Our clothes are quickly discarded as we backpedal towards the sofa, indulging in sensual kisses and tantalizing licks.

"Lay down," I whisper in her ear, and she eagerly complies, pulling me down with her. Our bodies entwine in a frenzy of desire as I explore every inch of her body with my hands and lips. As our breathing becomes heavy, I pause to appreciate her beauty. Her breath quickens, and her eyes meet mine.

I kiss her tenderly, starting with her forehead and working my way down her neck and shoulder. Her skin feels warm against mine, fueling the passion between us. I delicately grasp her brown nub between my fingers and bring it to my mouth to savor its taste while sucking on it, eliciting a gasp of pleasure from her lips. I explore her body with my tongue, tracing every curve and crevice and waking every nerve in her body. Trailing soft kisses along her stomach and thighs, her body shudders beneath my touch. I spread her legs further apart, the scent of her arousal stimulating my senses. As I lower my lips to her skin her breath hitches with each kiss, and she arches her back in response. I have Reign right where I want her. Her hands grip the cushion tightly as I dive my tongue into her, licking, sucking, and tasting. Reign's moans grow louder and more urgent, her hands now gripping my head as she writhes in pleasure. I focus on her preference, circling my tongue around her clit, savoring the way she trembles and gasps with each flick. I slurp up every drop of her essence before inserting my two fingers, feeling her muscles tense and release around it. I alternate between tongue and fingers, pushing her closer and closer to the edge of climax. With each thrust, she cries out in ecstasy, her body quivering against my tongue until she finally arches her back and releases a shuddering breath. As she comes down from her high, I gently kiss my way back up her body, enjoying the taste of her on my lips. I'm not finished with her yet.

"Turn around," I demand.

I position myself behind her as she gets on her hands and knees. With a firm grip on her hips, I slowly enter her from behind. The sensation of her tightness around me causes a low growl to escape from my throat. She is so wet, and I revel in the way she moans. She pushes back against me, urging me to go deeper, faster, and harder. I oblige, picking up the pace and setting a rhythm that has her gasping and trembling with pleasure. Her moans grow louder with each thrust, and I squeeze her ass cheeks as I continue to drive into her. Reign's nails dig into the sofa as she arches her back. I lean my chest against her back and reach for her aching clit rubbing it in circular motions while thrusting harder inside her.

"Yes, just like that," she gasps, her voice strained with delight.

Her body quivers beneath mine, and her muscles tighten as she cries out my name in pure bliss. Feeling her inner walls clench around me pushes me over the edge, and a surge of euphoria washes over me. I pull her in for a sloppy kiss, our tongues entwined, as we slowly come down from our shared release. We collapse together in a sweaty, satisfied heap, our bodies entwined in the blissful aftermath of our passionate lovemaking.

"Damn," she says, her voice still thick with desire, and my lips curl into a satisfied grin.

She rests her head on my chest, and my finger draws lazy circles on her back.

"You were holding back on me before, weren't you?" She nuzzles closer to me, her warm breath tickling my skin.

"Maybe a little," I admit with a chuckle.

She looks up at me, curiosity shining in her eyes. "So, did you mean what you said at the wedding about when we were playing ball?"

I gently lift her chin with my finger, meeting her gaze with a soft smile. "Every word," I reply, leaning in to capture her lips in a tender kiss. As we pull away, I brush a strand of hair behind her ear and say, "I meant every word then, and I mean it now. Reign, I've wanted you since May 8th, when I first saw you in that purple dress at the bar."

Reign's eyebrows furrow slightly, and her lips part in surprise as she remembers that night. "What do you mean?"

"I mean, the first time I saw you was on your birthday, at the Fifth Ave bar," I confess.

Her eyes widen, and a faint blush creeps onto her cheeks. "You were there that night?"

A smile playing on my lips, I nod.

Reign laughs softly. "Okay, since we're being honest and having a heart-to-heart, I remember you from that peanut butter commercial," she says, laughing. "You were every girl's childhood crush back then."

My smile widens. "I knew it!"

"Yum, that's good," we say the catch phrase from the commercial in unison, laughing.

When Reign catches her breath, she looks at me with a twinkle in her eye and says, "I was feeling you too when I first saw you, but I really fell for you when you kissed me in front of my cousins at family dinner…" She trails off, blushing slightly. "It felt sincere and right."

"It was, Reign," I assure her. "I realized early on that I was falling for you, but I was too scared to admit it because I wasn't sure how you felt. I thought this was just a business arrangement for you."

Reign smiles, shaking her head. "No, it wasn't just business for me," she says softly. "We probably should have just been honest with each other from the beginning of our fake relationship—"

"You mean *professionalship*," I correct her with a playful smirk.

She gives me a pointed look and giggles. "Yeah, that. We should have just been honest with each other from the start instead of waiting this long." Her hands roam up to my face, cupping my cheeks gently, and she adds in a low, seductive voice. "We could have been doing this a lot sooner."

My dick hardens at her touch. Clearing my throat, I respond with a husky tone, "Um, I tried to tell you months ago. You kept—"

"Water under the bridge." She cuts me off, placing a soft kiss on my lips. "We're past that now, and besides, I think the wait was worth it." Her lips brush against mine as she pulls back slightly. "Don't you agree?"

"Definitely worth the wait," I murmur, firmly gripping her waist and positioning her onto my erect member. With my hands firmly planted on both sides of her hips, I slide her up and down, feeling her warmth and wetness envelope me.

Her breath hitches meeting my thrusts with equal fervor. Our bodies move in perfect sync, melding together in a dance of passion and desire, and our heavy breathing intensifies as we reach a peak of pleasure once more. The desire that runs through me has never been so strong for any woman. We succumb to the waves of pleasure, and she rides out her aftershocks, her body trembling in response. We both catch our breath and embrace the peaceful slumber that follows.

The morning sun streams through the windows. I groggily open my eyes and reach out to pull Reign closer to me, only to find that she is no longer there. Rubbing away the remnants of sleep from my eyes, I realize I'm on the sofa, covered in a thin blanket. As I sit up, I hear the sound of running water coming from the bathroom, and I smile, knowing Reign is just on the other side of the door. I stretch my arms above my head, my morning erection tenting the thin fabric of the blanket. My pent-up sexual desire for Reign has been building for months, and I can no longer control my impulses. I quickly get up and make my way to the bathroom, knocking on the door.

Reign's voice calls out, "Come in!" I push open the door, and the steam from the shower fills the room. I catch a glimpse of Reign's silhouette through the frosted glass.

"May I join you?" I ask politely, pulling open the shower door and stepping inside.

Reign turns to face me, a sly smile playing on her lips as she nods in approval.

The warm water cascades over us, instantly relaxing my muscles. As I reach for the soap, Reign's hand brushes against mine, sending a jolt of electricity through me. Our eyes meet in the steamy haze.

"Let me," she says, taking the soap from my hand and lathering a washcloth. She begins to gently cleanse my body, paying special attention to my cock.

I groan, a grin forming on my lips. "Reign, baby, what are you doing?"

She continues rubbing me down. "I'm washing my man," she purrs, her voice low and sultry, which sends me over the edge.

I grip her waist, pulling her closer to me as the water continues to flow over us. She drops the washcloth as I trace my tongue along her collarbone, feeling her shiver in response. I gently push Reign against the tiled wall and lower my head between her thighs, throwing her leg over my shoulder as I devour what's mine. She gasps, her hands gripping my shoulders as she arches her back in pleasure, her nails digging into my skin. I delicately flick my tongue in and out of her, relishing the way she responds to me, her breath coming in short, ragged gasps. The sound of her pleasure drives me to intensify my movements, wanting to bring her to the brink of ecstasy. I focus on her sensitive spot, alternating between gentle licks and firm sucks, until she cries out my name in an orgasmic release, her body trembling with the force of her climax. As she catches her breath, I insert my fingers, curling them just right to send her over the edge once again.

Standing over her, I watch as her eyes flutter open. "I want you to come for me again," I order, my voice husky with desire.

She nods, surrendering to my command, her body still buzzing with the aftershocks of her first orgasm. My thumb circles her swollen clit as I continue to thrust my fingers inside her, feeling her walls tighten around them. With each movement, she moans louder. I can feel Reign getting closer, her breath quickening, and her body tensing. As she reaches the peak of ecstasy once more, I increase the pressure on her clit, pushing her over the edge into a second powerful orgasm. My pleasure comes from pleasing her. The way her body responds to my touch and the way her moans grow louder with each thrust only fuel my desire.

Reign grabs my shaft, stroking it slowly and tantalizingly, her mouth sucking on my neck as she whispers, "My turn."

My control slips away as she takes the lead, lowering herself to her knees and guiding me into her mouth, her eyes locked on mine as she takes me deeper.

"Fuck," I groan as she expertly swirls her tongue and sucks my dick like a lollipop.

My hand tangles in Reign's hair, her skilled mouth pushing me to the edge. She traces circles around my shaft while bobbing her head up and down, licking and sucking. She picks up the pace until the sensation overwhelms me. Reign deep throats me, nearly gagging until I release with a shudder.

"Shit, Reign!" I groan.

Reign swallows, her eyes never leaving mine, a satisfied smirk playing on her lips as she stands back up. I collapse against the tile wall, my legs feeling like jelly as I catch my breath. Reign rinses off under the water, and I watch as the droplets cascade down her smooth skin. I join her under the warm water, pulling her close. When our lips meet, the world fades away, and all that exists is the connection between us.

After our shower, we dry off and head to the bedroom, snuggling up together under the covers.

"I'm falling for you, Reign Brown," I admit, gazing into her eyes with sincerity.

She smiles softly, her eyes reflecting the same sentiment as she replies, "I'm falling for you too, Dion James."

We lay there in each other's arms until we drift off to sleep. I never would have thought that this fake relationship would turn into something so real and beautiful.

But here we are. Although I am not exactly where I want to be professionally, I am exactly where I need to be personally—loving Reign.

The End

If you have enjoyed reading this story, please consider leaving a review on Amazon, Bookbub, Goodreads, Fable, Storygraph or anywhere you can. It is extremely important for Indie Authors, even if it's just a rating. Please help spread the word.

This story can be read as a standalone; however, there is a book two.

Keep reading for the sneak peek at Chapter 1: Reign *"Is Love Enough?"* from the Love & Reign Series.

Wednesday
January 1ˢᵗ, 2025

Chapter 1: Reign

As the clock strikes midnight, New Yorkers erupt in cheers on my television screen, filling my room with the sounds of fireworks and celebration. Unlike previous New Year's Eves with Scarlette, when I was drunk on champagne and living my single life to the fullest, this year we spent it with our men, and I couldn't be happier. Dion and I enjoyed our first New Year's together watching the ball drop on TV while sipping champagne and cuddling on the couch. Scarlette and Eddie are still going strong, and I love that for them. And, of course, August rang in the New Year with her husband, Calvin. They are such a perfect match.

The six of us spent Thanksgiving and Christmas together and had the best time. My sister and her new husband, Peter, are still enjoying the honeymoon phase of their marriage, as far as I know. She hasn't returned any of my calls or texts lately, so I'm guessing they're just caught up in newlywed bliss, like Dion and me, although we are not married. While this is new for both of us, we are in a really good place right now, and I want to stay in this moment a little longer before shit hits the fan.

The last time I saw Skylar and Peter was at the Christmas Eve party my mother insisted on throwing. She forced me and Dion to attend, and being the bitch that she is, she also invited Max and his new wife. It was awkward, to say the least, but fortunately, Max kept to himself. The evening was bearable; however, now that Dion and I are officially together, I haven't spent as much time with my family. *What's the point?* My family is full of hostile, manipulative, and toxic individuals who only bring misery into my life. I used to justify their behavior because they were family, but now I realize I don't have to tolerate their disrespect. I'm just sorry it took me so long to realize that. *I could have cut ties with them years ago.* My mother made it clear that she was the one who brought me into this world and could take me out. She instilled in me that no one else would *care* for me as much as she and my family did. My father reinforced the idea that we are all we have and that, no matter what, we are family. He was an only child, and his parents were as well, so looking back, I can understand why he held onto that belief so strongly. However, my therapist has taught me that it is okay to love my family from a distance, and Dion, too, played a significant role in my decision to distance myself from them. He has nothing to do with the toxic members of his family. He explained that we are taught from a young age to believe that the poisonous traits in our families are normal and that we are simply expected to bend the knee and perpetuate the generational curse. His parents chose to break the cycle, showing that there's no need to keep in touch with a family member who isn't adding positivity to your life. Dion's example has shown me that when it comes to my cousins, fuck those bitches!

"Happy New Year, babe," Dion says, planting a gentle kiss on my lips, and a warm sensation travels down to my labia.

I am so in love with this man!

Who knew that three months ago, Dion and I would take our fake relationship to the next level? When he tore up the checks and confessed to me that he had wanted me since the first time he laid eyes on me, my heart leapt out of my chest and into my hand. I never expected to fall for Dion Atom James, but here I am, head over heels for him.

Looking up at him, my lips curl into a smile. "Happy New Year, my love."

He rests his forehead against mine and says, "I love you, Reign," making my heart swell with happiness.

"Show me how much you love me," I whisper, undoing the buttons of his shirt and tossing it aside.

With a mischievous glint in his eyes, he effortlessly scoops me up and throws me over his shoulder. I squeal as the glass of champagne in my hand spills on me, the bubbles trickling down my shirt. He chuckles, carrying me to the bedroom while holding the bottle of champagne in his other hand. As he gently sets me down on the bed, his eyes darken at my wet shirt clinging to my body.

"Let me take care of that for you," he says huskily, lifting the wet fabric over my head and leaning in to lick the champagne from the crevices between my breasts.

I close my eyes, surrendering to the wetness of his tongue, as a wave of goosebumps follows in its wake. Dion continues to trace his tongue along my collarbone and then to the curve of my neck, gently sucking as my breath hitches in my throat. His hungry eyes meet mine, a sly smirk playing on his lips. Anticipating what's to come next, Dion grabs the bottle of champagne, pouring the rest over my exposed skin. I shiver as the cool liquid trickles down my body, contrasting with the heat of his mouth on me. With each lick, I gasp and squirm beneath him until every droplet of champagne has been licked clean. My breathing becomes shallow as he firmly sits me up, reaching behind me to unclasp my bra. My breasts spill out, my nipples hardening under his gaze. Dion captures one of my nubs between his fingers, pinching and rolling it between his thumb and index finger, sending a jolt of pleasure straight to my core. I bite my lip, trying to stifle a moan as he lowers his head to take my nipple into his mouth, sucking and swirling his tongue around it. The sensation is overwhelming, and my body reacts instantly as fluid pools between my thighs.

My hands grip onto his shoulders, my nails digging into his skin. "Dion!" I cry out.

His movements become more urgent, and with a single, quick motion, he slides my shorts and lace underwear off. A gasp escapes my lips as he tugs me closer, his mouth between my legs and his tongue expertly flicking against my pulsating clit. I toss my head back, breathing in short gasps. With each lick and lap of his tongue, I feel myself teetering on the edge of ecstasy.

"You taste even better than champagne," Dion growls, stopping to lay on his back and pulling me on top of him. "Sit on my face," he commands, his hands gripping my hips.

I comply, straddling his face and riding his tongue until my body shudders with waves of ethereal pleasure. I throw my head back and shut my eyes, enjoying the sensation of his skilled mouth on me. He flips me onto my back and continues his expert motions with a satisfied smirk on his face. He inserts two fingers inside me, thrusting in and out, and uses his other hand to stimulate my clit pushing me over the edge once again. My soft moans turn into louder cries as I reach my peak, my body trembling and every fiber of my being feeling alive and electrified. My hands clutch at the sheets, and I stare up at the ceiling, my chest rising and falling rapidly as I catch my breath, until I finally come back down to earth from my second orgasm.

"I could eat you out every day," he murmurs in my ear, and I roll on top of him to return the favor.

"My turn," I whisper back, and he helps me slide off his jeans and boxers before I straddle him, feeling his hardness pressing against me.

Lowering myself onto him, I clamp my mouth shut to stifle my moans as he guides me with his hands on my hips, setting a rhythm that has us both gasping. I ride him harder and faster, relishing the sound of our skins slapping together.

"I want you to shout my name, Reign," he groans, his grip on my hips tightening.

My pussy squeezes around his girth, refusing to let him have the upper hand. With a smirk, I lean down to his ear and whisper, "Make me."

His eyes darken with desire as he spins us over to doggy style, fully aware that's my favorite position.

"Let me hear you say it," he groans, squeezing my ass and thrusting deeper and harder into me and hitting all the right spots.

Throwing my ass back, I am unable to contain my pleasure any longer and scream his name.

"Diooonnnn!" I shout at the top of my lungs.

"Yes, just like that," he growls, his movements becoming

more intense at the sound of his name on my lips. I grip the sheets tight as he continues to drive me wild with each powerful thrust. Aware that he's getting close, I match his rhythm. With a final thrust, Dion lets out a guttural groan as we both reach the peak of ecstasy together, our bodies trembling in unison before collapsing in a tangled heap of limbs and heavy breathing.

We stare up at the ceiling, our chests rising and falling.

"I don't think I've ever had that many orgasms before," I admit breathlessly.

Dion's lips curl into a sexy smile. "Well, I aim to please, and I'm glad I could deliver," he replies, his voice deep with satisfaction.

I bite back a blush and playfully swat his chest. "Oh, shut up!"

He chuckles, pulling me closer and planting a soft kiss on my forehead. Snuggling into his arms, I bask in the soft glow of moonlight filtering through my lavender curtains. Dion holds me tight, his steady heartbeat against my ear, lulling us into a peaceful sleep.

This was definitely the best New Year's I've ever had.

Thank you for reading the sneak peek of *"Is Love Enough?"*

For this story we will be digging deep within their relationship.

Please refer to my website for a more detailed list of the content warnings for book two.

Author's Note

Thank you for purchasing Loving Reign, I hope you have enjoyed my story as much as I enjoyed writing it.

Let's be friends!

Please find me on any of the social media platforms below and join my newsletter.

My website: https://kcmcmillian.mailchimpsites.com/

Newsletter: https://eepurl.com/iJtSzA

Instagram: www.instagram.com/kcminspired_author

My Broadcasting Channel on Instagram:

https://ig.me/j/AbbtqGM3rQEE4wwD/

Facebook: www.facebook.com/kcmcmillianauthor

Facebook Group:

https://www.facebook.com/groups/931639820833941/

TikTok: www.tiktok.com/@kcminspired_author

GR:

www.goodreads.com/author/show/22481124.K_C_McMillian

Books by K.C. McMillian

<u>*Young Adult Fantasy:*</u>

- <u>Bright A Forbidden Love Story</u> (second edition), available now.
- <u>Seventeen Magic is Real Part I.</u>, available now.
- <u>Earth Magic is Real Part II.</u>, available now.
- <u>Magic is Real: Seventeen & Earth Hardcover Special Edition</u>, available now.
- Fire & Ice: The Toussaint Sisters (TBA)

<u>*Adult Romance:*</u>
Intended for readers 18+ & older.

- <u>Loving Reign: A Fake Dating Romance Story</u> (Book One) available now.
- Is Love Enough? (Book Two of Love & Reign series) (TBA)

<u>*Adult Fantasy:*</u>
Intended for readers 18+ & older

- The Forbidden Fruit: Tales of the Remi Clan (The Nosis Series) (TBA)

Acknowledgments

Thank you so much for purchasing my book; I really hope you enjoyed reading Reign and Dion's story. I really appreciate you for taking a chance on my book; it means the world to me.

I want to express my gratitude to my mother for giving me the opportunity to share a part of her breast cancer journey in my book. In fifth grade, the news hit me like a ton of bricks: she had breast cancer—the gravity of the words weighed heavily on me at that moment. I had no idea what that meant for her or our family. But one thing I did not see was *fear*. I'm not sure if you hid it from me or what; however, you didn't cry, or at least I didn't see it. The day I noticed your hair falling out was traumatic for me, and I started crying. You smiled and said, *"Baby, this is just hair. It will grow back."* Although you were so strong, I cried because I didn't know what would happen. Twenty-three years later, you are still here, and I am grateful to God for that. I love you!

While writing this story, I was overcome with so much happening in my life: death, disappointment, and sicknesses, to name a few. I was ready to give up on this writing thing altogether. However, there were a few people that pushed me to keep going. I apologize in advance if I have missed anyone. Caron, Louise, L.C., E.C., Tonna, Mirna, and Zowie. Thank you all for your encouraging words, advice, and support during this challenging year when I know you all were going through something of your own. I thank all of you for that.

Troy, my husband, I love you with all my heart. Thank you for being such a good husband and incredible father to our little ones.

Thank you for being there for me during my many many breakdowns. I really don't know what I would have done without you by my side. Love you, babe.

Shalinie, thank you for joining me on this journey again. I don't know what I would do without you. Thank you for including my writing schedule in your busy life, always coming through with advice, and helping to make my stories even better. Thank you for listening to all my crazy ideas over and over again and being there for me when I change my mind. I truly love and appreciate you!

Alicia, thank you so much for joining me on this crazy ride. I never thought when I first asked you to proofread my story that you would be with me three books later. It's wild how a job we both no longer work for created such a bond between us. Thank you so much for your support and for adding my book schedule to your busy life. Thank you for taking on the role of my proofreader and always coming through for me, making my stories even better. I love and appreciate you.

Amy, my bestie, my sister from another mother and father. Haha, I love and appreciate how supportive you have been. I swear there are days where I am just like, I don't know what I would have done if I didn't have you to speak to. Thank you for being a part of my "unpaid team" and for listening to my crazy ideas all the time. Thank you for coming up with the name for my series (Love & Reign) and for your crazy one-liners that end up in my stories. Thank you for inspiring my over-the-top and hilarious characters; I swear we have the funniest conversations, which sometimes end up in the story. Thank you for always sharing my books and doing everything you can to spread the word. I could literally go on and on, but I'm not. I love and appreciate you so much!

Fab, my sister, thank you for your immeasurable support over ten years. I thank you for always being there for me and your advice and ideas. Thank you for allowing me to bounce around ideas with you and thank you for coming up with the title "Is Love Enough?" you are truly unique. Thank you for allowing me to vent about my lack of sleep and everything in between. Thank you for being you! I love and appreciate you forever!

About the Author

When Kiana "K.C." McMillian was a child, she would make up stories in her head and write them down. While attending high school, her favorite play was Romeo and Juliette, and she enjoyed reading it, but she sometimes fumbled over her words while reading in front of her classmates. And, of course, children can be cruel. Kiana didn't like being made fun of and lacked confidence in herself, and she felt that if she couldn't read in front of a crowd, then perhaps she wasn't good enough to write. She didn't think her stories would be well received and feared failing at something she loved. Kiana knew back then that she would one day want to share her imagination with others, but she wasn't sure about putting herself out there.

Fast forward twenty years later, after the death of her husband's grandmother on January 13th, 2022, she decided she wouldn't let the fear of failure hinder her from following her dreams. Before "Gran," as she and her husband called her, left this earth, she said, "I have lived my life, and I've done everything I wanted to do; I'm ready."

K.C. knew that if her life suddenly came to a tragic end, she wouldn't be satisfied. That statement inspired her, and she decided to follow her dream of becoming an author.

www.ingramcontent.com/pod-product-compliance
Lightning Source LLC
Chambersburg PA
CBHW020024310726

48970CB00007B/2197